CRIME OF MAGIC

DRAGON'S GIFT THE DRUID BOOK 2

LINSEY HALL

For Pam & John.

1

—————

"Oh fates! Hide here!" Panic flashed inside me as I grabbed my two sisters' arms and dragged them into a nook in the castle wall. I pressed against the wall, my breath held.

Bree and Rowan crowded against me, smooshing me into the cold stones. We squeezed behind a statue, mostly concealed.

"Why are we hiding?" Rowan asked.

"Potts is coming," Bree whispered.

She'd seen the day librarian, too. And probably sensed him with her amazing hearing. The *last* thing we wanted was to run into the crotchety day librarian right before we snuck into the library and broke into a secret tunnel.

My sisters and I stood still as statues as we waited for him to pass. Bree's dark hair fluttered into my mouth, and it took all I had not to spit the flyaway strands out.

It took Potts ages to pass, since he was older than the crypt keeper. I tended to like older people, but Potts was so grumpy you'd have thought someone put cement mix in his morning coffee. Every morning.

Through a gap in the statue, I saw Potts shuffle by, grumbling about Florian moving the books into the wrong places. He had an ongoing feud with the night librarian, and they fought like two cats over a catnip toy.

Except not *nearly* as cute.

When he finally passed, my shoulders relaxed. We gave him a minute more, then moved to slip out of the nook.

The sound of voices stopped us, and we pressed ourselves farther into the shadows.

Two people were walking down the hall, chattering away.

"I don't buy it," said a feminine voice. "No way she stopped the cloaked figure from stealing the spell."

"I've seen her in class," said a guy. "She's a disaster."

I stiffened.

There was only one person they could be talking about.

Me.

Shit.

"Probably just made it up," Lavender said. It had to be her, my fellow institute trainee. She hated me. "Who knows *what* she gave Lachlan Munroe in order to get him to agree to her story."

"Oh, I think I know," Angus said. He always hung around Lavender, so it had to be him.

She snickered.

Rowan started to move, then Bree. I grabbed their arms, not wanting them to get in a fight on my behalf.

A second later, Lavender and Angus passed. I held tight to Rowan and Bree for a moment more. Bree could crush them with her power, and Rowan's magic might be gone, but she could fight like a demon.

"They're such jerks," Rowan muttered.

Yep. And they were my classmates. I clenched my teeth, determined not to care.

Bree turned to me, concern in her eyes. "You're doing that stiff upper lip thing, aren't you?"

"Keep calm and carry on, right?" I said.

"It's your specialty." She frowned. "But you know you can be pissed, right?"

"Being pissed means I care," I said. "I don't care. I *can't* care." I still had bruises from our last magical combat class. Those two had used their offensive magic to beat the crap out of me, and with my shield magic on the fritz, I'd pretty much just been a piñata.

If I cared, I'd be an idiot.

Everyone else at the Protectorate had been impressed when I'd helped Lachlan Munroe stop a mysterious cloaked figure from stealing a dangerous spell last week.

Not those two.

It'd just stoked their dislike.

Whatever. Can't win 'em all.

"Come on," I said. "Let's go."

We slipped out of the nook, into the wide hallway. It was one of the older passageways in the castle, and the walls were ancient stones that had seen hundreds of years of activity. Warm candlelight from the sconces gleamed on the old wooden floors. We'd only been here a few months, but I loved this place.

Who wouldn't love living in a castle?

"I know it's fine if we're out at night." Rowan pushed her dark hair over her shoulder as her eyes gleamed blue in the low light of the wall sconces. "But I really *don't* want to run into Potts again. If that means cowering behind a statue, so be it."

"Amen, sister." I nodded.

Mayhem, Bree's ghostly sidekick, fluttered in the air up ahead. The little pug glowed a transparent white, her small wings working overtime to keep her aloft. She peered around the corner and then looked back at us, wagging her tail.

It was our signal that the coast was clear.

We kept going, moving silently along the hall.

I had to agree with Rowan—there wasn't much need to

sneak around. I didn't think we were doing anything wrong. Even though this was the Undercover Protectorate's school of magic, we were all adults.

But it was more fun to sneak through the halls at night, led along by a ghostly pug with a fondness for ham.

Anyway, Rowan was right. The last thing *anyone* wanted was to piss off Potts.

We reached the library without any more incident and slipped inside. Shelves lined the walls that towered high above, stuffed full with leather-bound books. The spines gleamed in the light of the fireplaces that burst to life upon our entrance. Paintings hung on the walls, some stacked right on top of books.

I grinned. The whole place was magical.

As usual, Chaos and Ruckus, Mayhem's two ghostly pug buddies, sat in a plush bed in front of the biggest fireplace. Probably waiting for Florian to read them their bedtime story.

What wasn't normal was the Cats of Catastrophe. The raga-muffin cat gang sat on a big wooden table, clearly up to no good. Princess Snowflake III, the fluffy white Persian who wore a diamond necklace, sat at the edge of the table, throwing daggers with her eyes.

"I think she's the lookout," Bree said.

"Oh fates," I sighed, watching as Muffin, the hairless black sphynx cat, tried to pry a gemstone out of a fancy lamp that sat in the middle of the table. A sapphire glittered in his tattered ear. A couple days ago, it'd been an emerald to match his green eyes. He'd changed out his jewelry.

I had no idea how he'd managed it, but he was the Cat Sìth, the most magical cat in Scotland, so he had a few tricks up his sleeve. Muffin was the leader of the gang, which specialized in stealing fish from the docks and organizing complicated jewel heists.

Beside him, Bojangles chewed on his tail. The goofy cat was paying no attention to the jewel heist in progress.

"Isn't this a bit amateur for you guys?" I asked.

Muffin glanced at me, his front claws still clutched around the jewel that he was trying to pry free. "Meow." *Everyone needs a hobby.*

"Fair enough, but how about you run your operation *out* of the castle. You're making me look bad." A little over a week ago, they'd followed me back here and never left. I didn't mind having feline sidekicks, but if they were going to steal stuff, it was no good.

Muffin gave an audible sigh, then lowered his claws. He looked longingly at the bright red stone, then at me.

"Go steal hams from the kitchen with Mayhem," I said. "No one seems to mind that."

I didn't give him time to answer. Who was I kidding anyway? He wouldn't listen to me.

"*Ooooooooh, ooooooooh.*" The ghostly wail echoed from the far wall.

I looked at my sisters and grinned.

"Wipe that smile off your face," Bree whispered.

I did, but it was hard.

"Who is it?" Bree asked in a tremulous voice.

We all knew who it was—Florian, the ghostly night librarian —but we played along anyway. He liked to scare people. Unfortunately for him, he was the least scary ghost in the history of ever.

"*Ooooooh, oooh.*" The wails came again.

I stifled a small laugh. "Terrible and tragic ghost, have mercy!"

Florian drifted out from the bookshelf, his fancy eighteenth century outfit making him look like he was about to go to a ball.

His wig sat slightly askew, the curls towering above his head. "I did quite a good job that time, didn't I?"

I nodded. "Superb. You really had my heart going there."

He smiled and bowed, then stood. "You're here for our mission?"

"Can't wait." I swung my arms over Bree and Rowan's shoulders. "I brought some backup."

He clapped. "Good, good!" With a sweeping gesture of his arm, he indicated for us to follow him, so we did, heading back to the older part of the library.

Last week, my new and uncontrollable magic had delivered a premonition that there was a trapdoor in the library—one that had been long forgotten. When Florian and I had gone searching for it, we'd found it. But it'd been locked tight. This was the first time we had a chance to investigate. I'd been busy trying not to drown in my classes.

It wasn't going so hot.

I pushed the thought away and followed Florian to the back wall. He led us toward a door hidden on the right side, and we followed him into the massive hidden library in the back.

As always, a sense of wonder filled me. The front library was incredible—I'd never say it wasn't—but the back library was like something out of my fantasies. Florian called it the ghost library because it was his domain, but it really looked it.

The space was ten stories tall, with a massive open atrium in the middle. We entered at the middle, so it was possible to see both up and down, which lent the place a feeling of majesty and grandeur.

Each level circled the atrium and was filled with books. The ceiling was domed, the glass allowing light to filter through. Since it always shined at all hours of the day, I had to assume it was magic. It glittered on the dust motes in the air, and glowing balls of light hovered near the ceiling.

"Come, come." Florian headed for the railing that bordered the open space in the middle. As he walked, the railing disappeared, and a staircase formed in its place.

The library only admitted you if it wanted to or if you'd earned it. I'd had to earn my way in last week by finding the long-lost trapdoor. Now we were going to figure out what was inside the door, and the library seemed to be totally down with this plan.

"I can't believe this place really exists," Rowan whispered as we walked down the sweeping staircase to the next level.

"Me neither." Bree and I had only been here about a month longer than she had, and we'd barely adjusted. It was still the most incredible place I'd ever been, and I was certain it would retain that title until the day I died.

"I've tried everything I can think of to pry the door open," Florian said. "But none of it has worked."

"What'd you try?" Bree asked.

"Well, pulling the handle, mostly." He shook his head. "Didn't work."

I stifled a small laugh. "Hopefully Bree can help us."

As a Dragon God, she'd been gifted with the powers of different Norse gods. One of those—super strength—had come from Magni, one of the sons of Thor.

"I do hope you're right." Florian led us around a tall bookshelf. "I desperately want to know what is in the door. It's as if the castle is trying to tell us something."

If it was, I definitely wanted to figure it out. This was Florian's domain, and I was just glad he'd invited us along.

He led us toward the back corner of one of the lower levels, where we'd found the trapdoor. It was set into the wooden floor in a forgotten spot in the library. The ancient rug and table that had once covered it were pushed up against the bookshelf behind it. I wasn't convinced we'd find anything interesting down there, but I sure as heck wanted to look.

Florian rubbed his hands together and peered down at it. "All right, get going!"

Bree saluted, then bent down and grabbed the round iron ring that was set into the wood. She pulled at it, yanking hard.

Nothing.

"Come on, don't be a wimp," Rowan teased. "Give it your all."

Bree's face turned red as she pulled, and sweat popped out on her brow. She was more than strong enough to lift a car, so this should be possible.

Unless...

"It's got to be magic," I said.

Bree dropped the chain. "I can't break through that."

"Dang." I rubbed my chin, then looked at Florian. "You've checked the library for any clues?"

"I have. Nothing."

Rowan bent over the door, inspecting. "And there's no keyhole."

I frowned. We had to figure out the spell that kept it locked.

"Try your new magic," Bree said. "See if it will tell you anything."

"I can try, but no promises." It'd been wonky as hell, lately. The new power had appeared about a week ago, and I still wasn't sure what it was. Normally, magical powers were obvious. Fire Mages threw fireballs, Telekinetics moved stuff with their mind, Seers could see the future when they tried.

But me?

Sometimes my new magic would answer questions I asked it. Sometimes it wouldn't. Since I was a Dragon God like my sister, the magic had to come from one of the mythical pantheons. But I had no idea which one.

I closed my eyes and focused on my magic. It was hard to find, almost like it lay dormant inside me.

Since it had worked when I'd asked it questions before, I tried that this time as well.

How do we open this door?

Crickets.

I squeezed my eyes shut tighter and tried to focus on my magic, but it was hard.

How do we open this door?

Nothing.

"Any luck?" Bree asked.

I opened my eyes. "Not now. I think I need to practice more."

But how? Lachlan, the irresistible shifter mage who haunted my dreams, had promised to help me, but I hadn't seen him in two days, since he'd asked for my help finding the cloaked figure who'd tried to steal a dangerous spell from him. We may have saved the spell from the thief, but we still wanted to catch him.

A loud, deep meow caught my attention, and I turned.

As if he'd heard me thinking about him, Lachlan had appeared, led here by Muffin, who sat in front of him.

I swallowed hard, trying to keep my cheeks from heating.

But *of course* all I could think about was our one kiss, and then the fact that Lachlan had said it couldn't happen again because we were now working together.

That kind of awkwardness was totally my style, but it didn't mean I'd gotten used to the sheer torture of it.

Lachlan's gaze lingered on me a moment longer than everyone else, then he tore his gaze away.

Honest to fates, it looked like he tore it away.

It could be my wishful thinking, but... Maybe not.

His gaze dropped to the trapdoor. "That looks interesting." Lachlan's Scottish accent was thick.

"It is." My voice came out totally not squeaky or awkward at all, and I counted it a major victory. "What are you doing here?"

"I had news, and Muffin was kind enough to lead me here."

"The library admitted you." Florian's brows rose, clearly impressed.

"Aye, if you mean that a staircase appeared."

"Hmmm." Florian nodded. "Interesting."

Muffin walked to the trapdoor and started scratching at it.

"Did you have any luck tracking the scrap of fabric from the thief's cloak?" I asked.

Last week, Lachlan had fought the thief while in his lion form. A scrap of fabric from the cloak had been torn off and stuck in his paw. It was our only clue.

Lachlan nodded. "I've found a tracking spell that will help us find him. It will take a couple days to start working—this potion takes time to brew—but then, we should know more."

Satisfaction filled me. *Good.*

The thief had stolen an *ancientus* spell, designed to bring back magic from the past. Usually, that meant dangerous magic. He might not have gotten away with the *ancientus* spell, but that didn't mean he was going to quit his evil plan. Whatever it was, we wanted to stop him.

Lachlan pointed to the door. "Do you need help?"

"Strength won't do it," I said.

"I'm more than just brute strength," he said.

Boy, did I know it.

He knelt by the trapdoor and touched the metal ring that was connected to the locking mechanism within the door. Soon, the ring glowed red hot, then it began to melt away, dripping through the hole in the trapdoor. Once it was all gone, leaving nothing but a hole in the wood, Lachlan stepped back.

"Hopefully that will break the spell," he said. "If the lock is gone, there can't be a spell on it, right?"

"Let's find out." I figured it had cooled enough, so I reached into the little hole where the iron ring had been anchored and pulled.

The trapdoor burst open. Stale air wafted out, and I stumbled back, covering my mouth to keep from breathing in the dust.

When it settled, we all stepped forward, peering in.

A pale blue light gleamed from within. Ancient stairs led deep into the castle. The air smelled of water and dust, a strange combo.

"Whoa," Rowan murmured.

"No kidding." Bree stepped onto the first stair, avoiding the cooling puddle of metal. "Let's check it out."

"Shouldn't we tell someone where we're going?" I said. "In case it's dangerous."

"Plan B?" Bree asked.

"I couldn't possibly wait." Florian drifted through Bree, who shuddered, and started down the stairs.

I shrugged, then followed. Between us, we had some mega power. And nothing could hurt Florian. If we got in a pickle, he could always go for help.

We hurried down the stairs, our footsteps silent on the stone. The blue light that glowed grew brighter as we went. It felt like forever that we descended, going deep below the castle.

The Protectorate was built on a massive cliff overlooking the North Sea, so there was plenty of space below ground.

"When was this built, do you think?" I asked.

"Never heard of it in my day," Florian said. "It's centuries old, at least."

Finally, we reached the bottom. The staircase opened up into a massive cavern. Blue luminescence glittered in the ceiling, dripping down to light the entire space with a ghostly glow. A lake sat in the middle, sparkling from the blue light above.

"Wow." The word rushed out of me on a breath. I'd never seen anything like this.

It was as if magic had come alive.

Except... "Do you guys feel any magic?"

"None," Lachlan said.

"Nothing." Bree frowned.

"That's weird, right?" Rowan asked. "You'd expect it, in a place like this."

"Yeah." I went left, exploring the walls of the cavern, looking for any clues about what this place was used for. My friends joined the search, pacing around the large space. I couldn't keep my eyes off the glowing blue lights that glittered in the ceiling, but eventually, I was drawn toward the lake in the middle.

The water looked black as tar where the blue lights didn't glitter on it. In the middle was a small island, upon which sat a pedestal.

"It's the most beautiful thing I've ever seen," Bree said.

"Agreed." I paced around the lake, eyeing the empty pedestal in the middle. I pointed to it. "That's weird, right?"

"There should be something on it," Lachlan said. "This place was built for it."

On the other side of the small lake, I found a strip of ground that led to the pedestal.

I raised my hand, igniting the lightstone ring on my finger, then hovered it over the skinny land bridge.

"What are you looking for?" Lachlan asked.

"I don't know. Footprints, maybe. I might be jumping to conclusions, but if something is supposed to be on that pedestal and it's not, then that means it's been stolen. And I don't want my footprints erasing whatever is here."

"Good thinking."

I glanced up and caught a smile on his face. It flattened out, as if he didn't want me to catch him smiling. Strange. I turned back to the ground to study it.

"There are no footprints," I said. "Almost like...brush strokes?"

"A broom, maybe?" Bree asked.

"Could be. Something to clear the path."

A deep meow sounded from the other side of the cavern. I straightened immediately, recognizing it as Muffin's *You gotta check this out* meow.

He meowed again, and I hurried toward him, finding him in a darkened nook in the cavern. He stood at a hollowed out tunnel, staring into the darkness.

"Holy fates." I stepped closer to the tunnel and studied the carved out sides of it. The stone was a lighter gray. Fresher.

"That looks newly made," Lachlan said.

"Oh boy." I turned to face the others. "I think someone has broken into the Protectorate."

2

For a few seconds, there was dead silence.

"Shouldn't that be impossible?" Rowan asked.

"They strengthened the defenses on the castle walls a couple months ago," Bree said.

It had been as a result of the bastards who had been hunting me and my sisters, but it had made the castle that much stronger.

"How long would it take to tunnel into here?" Florian said. "We're hundreds of feet deep. And this is solid stone."

"Depends on what kind of magic you have," Lachlan said.

I leaned against the wall, my mind racing. Someone had actually broken into the Protectorate. Recently.

I hurried toward the land bridge again, wanting to see if I could find anything at all.

My friends followed, stopping along with me at the bridge that led to the pedestal in the middle. It was glaringly empty.

I turned to Bree. "Can you fly over the land bridge, see if you notice anything?"

I knew we needed to alert Arach and Jude—the rest of the

Protectorate—but this would only take a moment. And I didn't dare walk on the bridge.

Bree nodded. Her magic filled the air, bringing with it the scent of cedar and the sound of a whistling wind, and her wings flared from her back, silver and bright.

A moment later, she was airborne, hovering over the land bridge, her face pressed nearly to it. She wore her own light-stone ring, which shed a golden glow on the dirt.

A few moments later, she returned, landing next to me. "Nothing. They brushed away all footprints."

I frowned. "There might be more clues, but we need to tell the others."

"Immediately!" Florian was extra pale, even for a ghost.

Lachlan was pacing around the chamber, Muffin at his side. They were clearly looking for clues.

"Come on!" I shouted to him. "We've got let the others know."

We all departed the chamber, racing toward the top. Muffin led the way, sprinting up the stairs on his skinny legs. My lungs were about to burst by the time we made it back into the library. Muffin darted off, and we followed.

Bojangles and Princess Snowflake III were still on the table in the main library. Princess had managed to pry the red jewel off and was now staring at it in delight. I ignored her, hurrying through the library and into the hall.

"I'm headed to Arach's room first." I turned right. The dragon spirit who'd given her magic to create this place didn't actually live at the castle, and she couldn't be called on command. But if she were going to arrive, it would be there, in her office on the main floor.

The halls were quiet as we ran. It was after eight at night, and anyone who'd finished working had probably gone to the

Whisky and Warlock, our favorite pub in Edinburgh. I just prayed that Jude was still here.

When I reached Arach's room, I didn't bother knocking. The door wasn't locked, but when I entered, it was totally empty and cold. Dead, almost. Normally, the room had life to it. There were dozens of colorful paintings on the tall walls, and the warm wooden furniture gleamed under the lamps.

But at that moment, it felt like it'd been empty for decades.

I turned to face my friends, dread opening a hole in my chest. "This seems wrong."

Bree's face was pale as she inspected the room. Rowan looked worried, and Lachlan was unreadable.

I turned back to the room. "Arach. We need you." I turned to look at Bree. "You said she came when you called once."

"I think she did. Or it was a coincidence." Bree's brow wrinkled. "Arach? We're desperate here."

We waited a few moments more, every minute lasting a lifetime.

"I don't think this is working," Lachlan said.

"We need to find Jude," Bree said.

"Agreed." I started toward the door, but it swung open.

In the hall, Muffin turned a corner toward us, followed by Jude and Hedy. The head of the Paranormal Investigative Team —the PITs, for short, which was truly a terrible acronym— walked in front of Hedy, the head of Research and Development. The lavender-haired witch looked concerned. Jude looked determined.

"Your cat brought us here," Hedy said.

"Any ideas why?" Jude stopped dead at the entry, her eyes widening as she studied Arach's office. "What has happened here?"

So she agreed. Something was off in Arach's office. "I don't know." Worry tugged at me. "But it might have something to do with a theft beneath the castle."

Jude's starry blue eyes met mine, and her brow wrinkled. "A theft under the castle?"

"We have to show you."

She nodded quickly. Jude was the head of the PITs for a reason. Cool under fire and one of the smartest strategists I'd ever met, she didn't dawdle in an emergency, that was for sure.

My heart raced as I led them all back down to the cavern beneath the castle.

"I had no idea this existed." Jude stepped onto the stairs leading from the trapdoor.

I showed her everything—the cavern, the pedestal, and the newly dug tunnel—and she didn't say a word. Hedy was silent, too, but her eyes darted everywhere, taking in every detail as concern and wonder flitted across her face.

Lachlan was silent throughout the whole process, quietly observing. He was an outsider here, not a member of the Protectorate or even a temporary staff member.

"We need to call all the department heads together," Hedy said. "We'll meet in the round room."

I wasn't surprised that we were meeting in the Undercover Protectorate's version of the war room. It was reserved for *Big Deals*. This was definitely a big deal.

Ten minutes later, I followed everyone into the round room. A huge circular table sat in the middle, though it was removed for big meetings when the whole Protectorate had to squeeze in. But for now, it was just the department heads, the investigators on the PITS, and those of us who'd originally found the cavern.

We were the first to arrive, but Caro, Ali, and Haris stepped into the room just a few minutes later. Besides Bree, they were the three other members of Jude's division. The one that I wanted to join.

Ali and Haris kicked a hacky sack between them, their dark hair glinting in the light of the wall sconces. The room was done in a medieval style, with stone walls, tapestries, and old-looking lights. I had a feeling that it hadn't changed since it was first built.

Caro flipped her platinum hair over her shoulder as she sat next to me. "You know what this is about?"

"Yeah," I whispered. "But better wait for Jude to explain."

The other department heads filtered in after the PITs. Letitia Hedwing came in first. I'd never spoken to her personally, but knew that she was in charge of the Interspecies Mediation department. There could be a lot of fighting amongst the supernatural species, and her calming presence probably did wonders for that.

Potts came in second, and the crotchety old day librarian shot me a look that could freeze iron.

Bree leaned close and whispered, "Whoops, I think someone figured out we broke into the library."

"Technically, we broke *through* the library," I whispered back, as I looked away from his angry gaze. "And we were in Florian's domain anyway."

"They fight over it."

"Men." I turned my gaze back to the door as Jesse Ammons entered. The leader of the Demon Trackers Unit was built like a football player, and no doubt he used that strength to take out plenty of demons who shouldn't be wandering the earth.

Technically, this was all way above my pay grade. As a student—and not an ace one at that—I shouldn't have been there. Nor should Rowan, who was even farther down the totem pole than I was. Lachlan might be a magical powerhouse, but he wasn't a member.

Except we were the ones who'd found the cavern, so there we were. And they couldn't pry me from my seat if they tried. I wanted to know what the heck was up. I felt like the castle had *asked* me to find that trapdoor when I'd had the vision of it.

"Why are we here?" Jesse asked.

Jude spoke first, explaining what we'd found under the castle. My gaze darted from face to face. Had any of them known it existed? From the looks of confusion and wonder, I'd give that a big fat *nope.*

"You're telling me that there's a massive cavern under *my* library?" Potts demanded.

"It's been there for many centuries," Florian said. "I don't know much, but I recall vague rumors from my day."

Considering that his day had been nearly three hundred years ago, this was old info. But with ancient supernatural caves, sometimes old info was the best info.

"What kind of rumors?" Jude asked.

"That Arach's magic was beneath the castle," Florian said. "Most of us knew that it was, and one scholar surmised that there must be a cavern there. To be honest, I forgot about it a long time ago."

Potts huffed. "Of course you did."

Florian's gaze shot to the old librarian. "Why you saddle-goose, what did you just say?"

"Gentlemen." Jude's commanding voice cut through the room as she raised her hands. "That's not helpful. Florian, continue."

"As you know, we have no record of how the castle was originally formed, other than that Arach gave her magic to create this place, back when she was a living dragon."

"No one has bothered to ask her?" Lachlan said.

Florian arched his brows. "We're not idiots, Arch Magus. We did ask her, but she didn't know. No one knew. That was the point. Her magic was so powerful that it was hidden by two other dragons—two older dragons who knew that their time was coming. The knowledge was lost with them intentionally, and because of that, it was protected. They didn't want anyone to find Arach's magic. Even she didn't know exactly where it was. Though she knew it was nearby, she didn't know the precise spell by which it was imbued within this place."

"That way no one could get the information out of her." Lachlan nodded. "Smart plan."

Magic swelled in the air, bringing with it a pale glow from the side of the room. I turned, squinting.

Slowly, Arach appeared. The dragon spirit was in her human form, but she was paler than normal. Dimmer.

"Arach!" Jude stood.

"Sit." Arach's voice was weak as she drifted over to the table.

"What's wrong?" Hedy asked. "You look weak."

"I am." She sank into an empty chair, her face drawn. "I think something is wrong. I feel...emptier."

Everyone at the table shared an uneasy glance. Normally, Arach was a powerhouse.

"You look faded," Jude said. "Weaker."

"I am."

"I think someone stole your magic from beneath the castle."

Arach's eyes flared wide. "Is that where my heart was hidden?"

"It seems most likely, yes," Lachlan said. "Especially given that you're experiencing weakness now."

"We should assume it was your magic," Jude said. "And that someone tunneled though the earth to reach it."

"This is very bad," Arach said. "The magic in my heart is what keeps my spirit here. Without it nearby, I will fade away soon. And the magic that hides the castle will go with me. Anyone will be able to find us."

Dread opened a hole in my stomach.

Not Arach.

Not the castle.

Jude nodded, her expression grim. "We need to find your magic quickly."

I leaned forward. "I want to help."

"You're still in training," Jude said. "You need to finish that."

"I was allowed to help Lachlan last week."

"Last week, *everyone* was involved because there were so many ways the clue could be interpreted. We'll put our best investigators on this. If we need more people, then you may be called in. But for now, you must continue your training."

"Enthusiasm will only get you so far," Hedy said.

I tried to keep the scowl from cutting too deeply into my face, but this *sucked*. Helplessness welled within me. "But I had the premonition that we'd find the trapdoor there."

"And if you have another one, let us know," Jude said. "But your magic hasn't been reliable lately, has it?"

"No." I bit the word out.

"It's because you *need to continue your training*. We can't risk your life when we have so many other skilled investigators. But I promise, if we need more hands on this, we will let you know."

Arach met my gaze. "It is for the best, Ana. You must become stronger, or the risk is too great."

I nodded stiffly, unable to argue with Arach, but it wasn't nearly over yet. If they were putting their best people on this, that meant Bree. She was on the PITs. I could help her.

"Caro, Ali, and Haris will get started on this," Jude said. "I'll help as well, and we'll call in some individuals from Ammons' Demon Tracker Unit."

"Not Bree?" I asked.

Jude's starry blue eyes met mine, as if she knew exactly what I was thinking.

"She's on a job to find a dangerous demon that is terrorizing Ireland."

Bree met my gaze. "I depart in the morning."

Dang.

"We'll have another meeting tomorrow," Jude said. "In the meantime, let's get to work."

I stood, my mind galloping away like a runaway horse. How was I going to get in on the investigation? Caro, Ali, and Haris were my friends, but they were also professionals. Jude had made it very clear what the score was, and they'd heard it.

"I'm going to rest," Arach said. "If I can think of anything helpful, you can find me in my office."

I studied her, my stomach twisting at the obvious weakness.

As everyone left, Jude caught my eye from across the room. "You'll be in class tomorrow night?"

"Definitely." I smiled, trying to make it look genuine.

She nodded, then turned to say goodbye to Ammons.

"You look like you just bit into a rotten banana," Rowan whispered next to me. Bree had already headed off to prepare for her trip to Ireland.

"You're saying I'm a bad fake?"

"The worst."

"I'll be sure to practice more."

Jude approached. "Rowan, could I speak to you a moment?"

"Sure." Rowan squeezed my hand. "I'll see you later, okay?"

"Yeah." I left her, striding out of the room and down the hallway, my mind pounding with frustration and a thwarted desire to help.

My magic was such a disaster, and it was holding me back.

I stormed out of the castle, picking up speed as I strode across the lawn. I just needed some breathing room. From the Protectorate, from people, from...myself.

I was the problem.

I was slow to master my magic, and this was the result. It was probably smart of Jude not to put me on this case, but I hated it.

I was the problem, and I couldn't outrun myself.

Desperate for some space, I followed the scent of the sea. The castle was built on a cliff overlooking the North Atlantic. Giant walls protected us on the land side, but the back was protected by a cliff that plunged hundreds of feet down to the sea. I could already hear waves crashing.

As I neared the stone circle that sat between the castle and the cliffs, I studied it. As always, I was drawn to it. Yet I hesitated.

There was something about that circle—something that attracted and repelled. I shivered.

Nope. Not going near something that felt like that.

I wasn't the type to ignore my instincts.

I skirted around the circle, catching sight of Muffin sitting on top of one of the towering stones. His eyes gleamed in the moonlight. The Cat Sìth looked right at home there.

He watched me pass. *Don't jump off the cliff.*

I shot him a one-fingered salute, and he grinned, fangs gleaming.

The crashing waves called me, and I hurried toward the cliff edge. The brisk sea wind blew my hair back from my face. I sucked in a steadying breath.

Slowly, my mind cleared.

"You're not going to jump, right?" Lachlan's voice startled me into a little hop.

I spun to face him. The moonlight gleamed on his dark hair. His cheekbones looked cut from glass, and he studied me, concern glinting in his eyes. Out here, in the middle of the Highlands, his tall, rugged build looked like a chieftain of old.

"Muffin already advised me not to," I said.

"Smart cat."

"Why did you follow me?"

"You seemed upset."

"You care?"

Concern and irritation flashed in his eyes, along with something I didn't recognize. "Of course I care."

I frowned. "All right."

I was being prickly. I knew it. But stopping it was hard.

"You're upset, then?"

"I'm pissed. Pissed at myself for not learning my magic sooner. With the fact that it's all weird and uncooperative and strange. Now there's a situation that I want to help with, and I'm held back. Half a supernatural."

"Half? Hardly. Untrained, maybe. But never half."

I didn't know what to say to that, so I went with nothing. The most I could manage was stewing over the cavern situation, anyway.

But why did I have to let them make decisions for me?

Sure, I wanted to become a full-fledged member of the Protectorate, but this was bigger than that. This was *Arach*. The heart and soul of this place. The magic that kept it running.

I had to help.

"What are you thinking?" he asked. "I can see the wheels turning."

"I'm thinking that Plan A was to ask them to let me help with this. Plan B is to take matters into my own hands."

He grinned.

"She didn't say I *couldn't* help. Just that I needed to finish my training."

"It was strongly implied."

"Thanks, Sherlock, I caught that. Doesn't mean I'm not going with Plan B. Gotta have a Plan B."

"You always have a Plan B?"

"And a Plan C. Fortunately, we're not there yet."

Lachlan nodded, as if he liked what he'd heard. "I'll help you."

"Why? You're already helping me learn my magic."

"Which we need to start immediately."

I nodded heartily. It was fair that the cloaked figure had been a priority. The FireSouls hadn't been able to help since the cloak had a blocking charm on it, but now that Lachlan's complex tracking potion was brewing, he had time. We needed to get on with the training.

"But why are you helping me?" I asked again.

"You'll be helping me find the cloaked figure when my tracking potion finally has a lead. I don't want you distracted by this." He hesitated, his expression softening just slightly. He'd have hidden that if he could. "And it's important to you."

"All right. Let's do it." I wasn't going to say no to that kind of help. Or any kind of help, really. "First step... I'm going back into the cavern."

"Should you wait until Jude's crew is done?"

"No time. I've got to be in class tomorrow, remember?"

"Fair enough." He grinned. "We'll be sneaky."

"We? You're starting so soon?"

"This is the best bit."

"All right, then. Let's go find some answers."

3

Lachlan and I headed back across the lawn as the moon shined bright overhead. We passed by the stone circle, and Muffin called out to us.

"Meow." *What fish are you off to smell?*

"Is that some kind of cat greeting?" I asked.

He gave me a look that suggested I was an idiot for not knowing, the sapphire glinting in his ear.

"Could you go scout the library, and when it's empty, meet me at the door?"

He gave a decisive nod, then leapt off the stone and streaked across the lawn toward the castle. The little gremlin was fast, and cute in his own skinny, hairless way.

"You have interesting friends," Lachlan said.

"Don't I know it."

We stepped into the massive entry hall, and I spotted Rowan heading up the stairs to our apartments.

"Rowan!" I called.

She spun, her eyes landing on me and Lachlan. They moved back and forth between the two of us, curious. I hadn't yet told her about the kiss because I knew both my sisters would heckle me to death, but she'd figure it out soon enough. We didn't keep secrets from each other. Not for long, at least.

She skipped down the steps. She wore all black, looking stark and beautiful with her jet-black hair and blue eyes. "Where were you?"

"Getting some air. What did Jude want to talk to you about?"

"She wants me to start training, even though my magic is still missing."

"Are you okay with that?"

She shrugged. "I'm better with my weapons than I've ever been." She was determined not to be helpless, even though she couldn't access her magic. "So yeah, I'm fine with it. I'm sure it'll kick my ass, but I want to contribute to my care and feeding."

I cracked a smile, but couldn't blame her. Even though Bree and I didn't mind taking care of Rowan while she got on her feet —she'd just recently escaped five years in captivity, after all— she was just like me. She wanted to take care of herself.

"Want to help us scout out the cavern beneath the library?" I asked. "We could use a lookout."

"Heck yeah. Let's do it." She spun her finger in a *let's go* motion, and we hurried off toward the library. I could always count on my sisters to be up for adventures.

The halls were quiet as we passed. No doubt the PITs had gotten a head start on us, and everyone else was asleep.

"Did you see how long ago the rest of the PITs went into the cavern?" I asked.

"I think they started right away. You going to tell them you're hunting?"

"No. Don't want to get them in trouble. I don't think they'll rat me out, but unless I have good info to give them to help them find a clue, there's no reason to put them on the line."

"Good idea."

Lachlan was our silent shadow as we made our way down

the old stone-lined hallway. The wide wooden floorboards creaked underneath our feet, and paintings of various supernatural creatures seemed to follow us with their eyes.

"Sometimes I still can't believe that we get to live here," I murmured.

"I know, right? Makes you want to pass the Academy and become a full member of the team."

"Ain't that the truth." Wistfulness whispered through me, followed quickly by determination.

I slowed as I neared the library, grabbing Rowan's arm to make sure she mimicked my action. "Muffin will be waiting out front if the coast is clear."

We slipped toward the side of the hall, near the nook where we'd hidden earlier. If we had to dart in there, we could hide.

As we neared, the door creaked open and Muffin slipped out.

"How the heck did he open that door?" Rowan whispered.

"The Cat Sìth has magic you can't imagine," Lachlan said. I glanced back to catch a sexy grin tugging at the corner of his mouth. "Mostly related to thievery, though."

"Opening doors falls into that category." I strode toward Muffin. "Thanks, pal."

"Meow." *Anytime, pathetic hunter.*

"Pathetic hunter?"

Why do you think Princess Snowflake III painted you the picture of the dead rat? Encouragement!

"Thanks." No way was I mentioning that I wouldn't start rat hunting anytime soon.

As quickly and quietly as we could, we made our way through the library. The Pugs of Destruction had departed their beds, no doubt to bunk with Bree, and the place was quiet. Muffin veered off toward the bejeweled lamp that was now short one red gemstone.

"Off for more loot?" I asked.

"Meow."

That was a definite yes.

As we approached the door that led to the ghost library, I caught sight of Florian. He sat in a chair in the corner, looking at his hand, a confused expression on his face.

"Florian? What's wrong?" As I stepped nearer, I realized what it was. "You're fading!"

He looked up at me, face stark. "I am."

Dread made my chest feel empty. "Arach's magic must help keep you here."

"It does." He nodded. "Oh, this is very bad indeed."

Shit, shit, shit.

We had to find Arach's heart before Florian faded away entirely. We'd lose more than just the magic that hid us from the world and allowed us to continue our work and live in peace. We'd lose Arach and Florian. Our friends.

"Don't worry, Florian. We'll find it."

He nodded, hope flashing on his face.

Determination fueled me as I turned, heading through the door toward the ghost library.

Fortunately, the library allowed us to use the stairs, making them appear before us when we entered the massive space.

"See? This is just evidence that the castle wants me to help," I said.

"Gotta say, I agree," Rowan said.

"Aye, I think you're meant to do this."

We made our way silently toward the trapdoor. I stopped behind a bookshelf, and the others followed suit. We peered through books. Two guards stood by the trapdoor. One chewed vigorously on a ballpoint pen, while another hummed lightly under his breath.

"Be ready to be quick," Lachlan whispered.

I barely felt his magic, though I knew he used it. Probably suppressing it so the guards didn't sense what was coming.

The one guard stopped chewing immediately, and the other ceased humming. They stood still as statues.

"Sprint past!" I whispered at Rowan.

Just like he'd done back in Paris, Lachlan had temporarily frozen time, so the guards wouldn't realize that we'd passed.

We raced by the guards, ducking low under their line of sight, then slipped down the stairs, deep into the earth. I kept my ears pricked for any sign that the guards had woken and sensed us, but heard nothing.

About halfway down, Lachlan whispered, "We're in the clear."

We made our way quickly into the cavern. It was just as magical as when we'd left. The glittering blue lights dripped from the ceiling, and the rest of the place was empty.

"I bet they're in the tunnel," Rowan whispered.

"Probably." I headed straight for the glittering pond that surrounded the pedestal, hoping to find something. Rowan and Lachlan spread out, and we searched the cavern for any clues.

When I turned up empty, I headed for the tunnel.

Lachlan was already there, inspecting every inch of the area where the tunnel met the cavern. He turned as I neared. "We'll have to go in."

I nodded, and stepped in. I heard nothing—no voices or footsteps. "I think the PITs are farther in."

"Good for us," Rowan whispered.

We crept quietly through the tunnel, which looked like it was freshly dug. Using what, though?

Like the cavern, it glowed with an eerie blue light from the glittering spots in the ceiling. About fifty yards in, a splatter of green slime on the ground caught my eye. It was about three feet around, and shards of glass were scattered around it.

"What's that?" Rowan whispered.

"Potion bomb, I think." I bent and sniffed it, but didn't dare touch. It looked like someone had taken a sample of it, complete with the dirt from below. "But I think it's important."

"Here." Rowan dug into her pocket and pulled out a plastic Ziploc bag. "Use this."

"Thanks." Rowan liked to be prepared. She also liked snacks. Which meant I wasn't surprised she had the little baggie on hand. I took the bag and bent down, then picked up a sample.

The sound of voices echoed in the cavern.

Crap.

They were close. Too close.

I met Rowan's startled gaze.

"Go!" she mouthed, then gestured down the tunnel, back into the cavern.

"What?" I mouthed back.

Then she turned and hurried toward the voices. Lachlan grabbed my arm and pulled hard.

I fought him, but he won, dragging me away. Rowan and Caro's voices echoed in the tunnel.

Rowan had taken the hit and covered for me.

Best sister ever.

Guilt tugged at me. I was grateful, but Rowan didn't deserve to get in trouble. Hopefully Jude wasn't with them, and Caro would cut Rowan some slack. She was a good storyteller. Liar, according to our Uncle Joe.

Lachlan and I raced through the cavern and up the stairs. He repeated the time-freezing trick, and we slipped by the guards, then through the library and out into the hall.

"I like your sister," Lachlan said.

I panted, trying to catch my breath after the long sprint. "I owe her big time."

"Can I see the sample?" Lachlan held out his hand.

I gave him the baggie, and he studied it, opening it to peer inside. To smell it. For a sec, I thought he was going to taste it.

Fortunately, he decided not to.

Unfortunately, his brow remained scrunched. "I've got no idea what this is, but we need to get out of here."

"Yeah, she won't rat us out, but they'll be coming up."

Lachlan raised his hand, and his magic swelled on the air, bringing with it the scent of pine and the sound of low thunder rolling in the distance. I shivered at the feel of a caress.

A gleaming silver light appeared in front of his palm. The light grew, bigger and bigger, until I could step into the portal.

I glanced at him. "Where am I going?"

"Don't you trust me?"

I wrinkled my nose as I stared at him. "Not sure that I do."

A sexy smile tugged at the corner of his mouth. "Magic's Bend."

"Good, I like it there." I stepped through the portal, letting the ether suck me in and spin me around, finally spitting me out on the street in Magic's Bend, the biggest supernatural city in America. There were only three, but this one in Oregon was the crown jewel.

I arrived just as the sun was dipping toward the horizon, sending a golden glow over the old factory buildings that lined the street in Factory Row. The city wasn't large—just over 60,000 supernaturals lived there—and this was the old factory district. Sometime in the last few decades, it'd been revitalized and turned into apartments and cool shops.

I stepped aside as Lachlan arrived, stepping through the portal next to me.

I eyed Potions & Pastilles, the magical coffee shop where my friends the FireSouls often spent their down time. "I assume we're visiting Connor to see if he can identify the potion?"

Lachlan's friend, who we'd rescued just a few days ago, ran

Potions & Pastilles along with his sister. He had a potions workshop in the back.

"Got it in one," Lachlan said. "I couldn't tell what it was, and while I could run some tests, I think it'd be better if both of us look at it. Two minds give us better odds."

I liked how he thought. Even though he was a super powerful mage and potion maker, he wasn't above asking for help. If there was one thing I'd learned in my years scrabbling to stay alive with my sisters, it was that help was often the only thing between me and failure. Or death.

So yeah, I was glad we were here to see Connor.

I peered through the golden script on the big glass window that said *Potions & Pastilles,* spotting a skinny dark-haired guy behind the counter. "I think we're in luck."

I followed Lachlan toward the coffee shop, stepping into a warmly lit space that was covered with local artwork. Mason jar lamps hung from the ceiling, and the whole place had an Oregon hipster vibe that I liked a lot.

In the corner, the FireSouls sat in their usual cluster of comfy chairs. Cass, Nix, and Del each had a glass in their hand as they waved at me. An enormous brown and white hellhound —heavy on the hound—sat next to Del. The dog lifted its ears, and its tongue rolled out. Pond Flower.

Potions & Pastilles turned into a bar in the evenings, and the FireSouls often came here to unwind. I would've to popped over to say hey, but there was no time.

Actually...

"I'll meet you at the counter, okay?" I said to Lachlan. "You can brief Connor."

"Aye, all right."

He strode off as I stepped toward the FireSouls, gingerly digging into my pocket for the plastic baggie that contained the gelatinous potion.

"Long time no see." Nix tucked her dark hair behind her ear, her green eyes glowing.

"Gee, what's it been?" I grinned. "Three days?"

"Too long." Del scratched Pond Flower's head.

"What have you got there?" Cass nodded toward the baggie, her red hair glinting in the light.

"A potion we're trying to track. We thought Connor could maybe identify it, but could you give it a look, too? See if you can sense where the owner might be?" FireSouls were capable of finding just about anything, as long as it wasn't blocked by a spell and they had a bit of information to spark their dragon sense.

"Got any info about it?" Nix hovered her hand out, ready to touch the bag.

"Nothing, unfortunately. Just that we found it in the Protectorate." Since those details weren't about the potion, it wouldn't help them. And even though I trusted them, it wasn't my place to tell them about the cavern under the Protectorate castle. That was Jude's domain, and I didn't need to step on it.

Nix blew out a sigh and took the bag, her face scrunched up. "I get nothing."

Cass took the bag from her and tried. "Nothing."

Del gave it her best shot last, but she just shook her head. "Sorry, pal. As far as I can tell, it's just some slime in a bag. We'd need a bit more to go on."

"Thanks though." I smiled to cover my disappointment. "Hopefully the potion master will have an idea."

"He's the best there is." Cass raised her can of PBR, the cheap beer that she adored. "And he's great at popping the top on a beer, too."

"So multi-talented." I grinned, but she was right. Connor really was the best. "I'll see you guys later."

I turned and headed toward the counter, picking up on the

sound of some old country playing over the speakers. Connor always chose the music for the shop, and often wore the band T-shirts to match his selection. Today, he wore a Lyle Lovett shirt.

I passed by a few college kids playing a game of checkers while drinking a golden liquid that looked expensive—how they afforded it, I had no idea—then passed an old man filling out a crossword puzzle while drinking a pink cocktail that steamed with a glittery smoke.

Connor grinned at me as I approached. "My favorite rescuer."

"Why thank you." I bowed. We'd really bonded while escaping the fortress-like winery in Tuscany last week. "Did Lachlan explain what we needed?"

"He did. I can give it a look now." He leaned back and shouted over his shoulder, clearly talking to someone behind the swinging door that led to the kitchen. "Sis? Can you take over?"

A moment later, Claire stepped through, her dark hair gleaming. She was wearing black leather from head to toe, and a sword was sheathed over her back. "I was just about to head out on a job."

In addition to helping out part-time at P & P, Claire was a mercenary. She killed demons most of the time, but every now and again, she'd be here.

"Just for a sec," Connor said, his British accent still thick despite the ten years he'd spent in America. "It's important."

"All right." Her gaze moved between me and Lachlan. "I can only assume it's a matter of life and death, if it's you two."

"Fair assumption." I glanced at Lachlan. That did seem to be the thing that brought us together. I didn't mind. My life had always been full of super dangerous situations, so adding in the company of a hot dude...

It wasn't the worst.

Even if I wasn't supposed to do anything more than look at him.

"Go on, then. I've got the counter." Claire took the apron from Connor, who led us back through the kitchen.

I followed him and Lachlan through the narrow space, toward the little workshop at the very back. It was cluttered with ingredients and vials and small cauldrons.

"Welcome to my domain." Connor spread his arms out wide.

"I like it." I'd never had the skill for potions—or the opportunity to practice, really—but I'd always loved the mad-scientist-looking lairs that most potion masters seemed to keep.

Lachlan and Connor hovered over the table, getting to work with a little cauldron, some flame, and a variety of bottles of colored liquid. I hung out near the back, watching as they tested various samples. Colorful plumes of smoke burst toward the ceiling, while the air filled with various scents—some nice, some definitely not nice.

I tapped my foot, anxious for a result.

"Getting impatient?" Lachlan asked without turning around.

"Um. No." Lachlan chuckled as if he could hear the lie. "Any luck though?"

"Maybe."

I waited a few more tense moments, until finally, Connor fist pumped the air. "Got it!"

"What is it?"

He turned, his eyes bright. Excitement gleamed within, but behind it was worry. "It's a Sylthian potion. They're really rare."

Lachlan turned. There was no excitement in his eyes, just worry. "Only a few people are strong enough to make it, and there are only a couple who are selling it. I can guess who made this, though."

"Who?" I asked.

"Torlock the Dark," Connor said.

I frowned. "Where's he live?"

"She." Connor shook his head. "And I don't know. I can ask around, but she's famous for being hard to get to."

"Then how do people buy her stuff?"

"They have to really want it," Lachlan said. "And it's so expensive that she doesn't need to sell a lot of it."

"What did that potion do?"

"It destroys a person's soul. They disappear forever. Just... poof," Connor said. "And there's no antidote, obviously."

A shiver of ice raced through me. "Holy fates. I carried that in my pocket?"

"It became neutralized once it sat on the ground for a few seconds. It's only good for a moment after it smashes into a person."

My shoulders sagged. Thank fates. And that was good for Caro, Ali, and Haris, too. If the potion was still active, I'd have had to warn them, and then Jude would know what I was up to.

"So someone must have dropped the potion bomb as they were running away from the cavern," I said.

Lachlan nodded. "Aye. Thieving cowards."

"We'll catch them." I frowned. "We just need to figure out where Torlock the Dark is. What kind of name is that, anyway?"

"Mega melodramatic," Connor said.

I glanced at the ornate old clock hanging on the wall. It was getting late. "I'm going to need to be at class soon. But we have to find Torlock."

Indecision tore at me. I couldn't skip class—Jude would kill me. The Protectorate was like a magical version of the FBI or Scotland Yard or whatever human crime fighting organization was the best. I had no idea. But I did know that rules were important, and Jude had looked me in the eye and asked if I'd be in class.

I'd said yes, and I wanted to live up to my promise.

But I also wanted to solve this damned crime.

"I have some contacts I can ask about Torlock," Lachlan said. "You go to class, and I'll do that."

"And I'll make some cocktails." Connor grinned. "Good luck, because I think you're going to need it."

4

As usual, I was getting my ass kicked in class. I'd managed a couple hours of sleep before it started, but it clearly hadn't been enough to prepare me for what was to come.

Not that I did much better when I was fully rested.

Today, I lay on my back, head spinning as I stared up at the enormous rafters overhead. Tweety birds flew in circles in the air above me.

I blinked.

Okay, that was my imagination.

Pain flared as I tried to stand. Lavender had really hit me with a big one. She was a telekinetic, and we were skirmishing. Unfortunately, she'd chosen to throw a huge wooden bench at me at the exact same time my shield magic faltered.

My core magical skill was really giving me hell these days, flickering in and out like an old lightbulb. It meant my Dragon God powers were coming to the surface—Maybe.

Aching, I dragged myself to my feet. On either side of me, two other pairs of students faced off.

But I only had eyes for Lavender.

Her dark hair gleamed in the light as she snickered at me. "I thought you were supposed to be someone special?"

I just scowled at her and tried to call on the magic inside me, begging my Dragon God side to come up with a new power. According to Bree, when she'd gone through the transition, new magic had just appeared out of the blue whenever she needed it. Times of strife called on gifts that could help. The Norse gods had heard her in her hour of need and delivered.

Whoever my gods were...they were clearly on lunch break.

All I had was a shoddy power of premonition and possibly some kind of light power that gave me...light. Honestly, I barely knew how to describe it, just that it had once appeared and driven off sickness wraiths.

"You really shouldn't be here," Lavender said under her breath, purple eyes glittering with pure donkey meanness.

"Matching your contacts to your name is a bit much, don't you think?" She was just a mean person, the type who liked to pick on the lowest one on the totem pole.

Unfortunately for me, that was my spot.

"You *and* your sisters shouldn't be here. Bree is a freak, and Rowan is worthless. No magic at all."

Hot tar seemed to fill my chest, spilling out at the mention of my sisters. It was fine if she wanted to be a bitch to me. But my sisters?

"Oh, no you don't," I said.

"What? You going to hit me with your practice sword?"

I growled at her. In skirmishes, I was allowed to use whatever I wanted to fight with. Since I had no offensive magic, that meant weapons. Unfortunately, Jude insisted on ones with no sharp edges.

"That's what I thought," Lavender said. "You're just as worthless as your sister Rowan."

Rage like I'd never known welled in my chest. It bubbled and boiled like a witch's cauldron, flaring out of me in a burst of light so bright that it slammed Lavender off her feet, throwing her into the wall behind her.

I felt like I'd been hit by a truck. All the wind was knocked out of me, and I stood there, my mouth open like a gasping fish.

Stunned silence surrounded me.

Lavender was still on her back, and everyone rushed toward her. Hesitantly, I stepped closer.

Angus, Lavender's friend, held up one hand, eyes flashing. "Don't."

I raised my palms. "All right."

I squinted at Lavender. Where was her hair?

Oh shit.

My light had blasted her hair away. And her clothes were singed, black and dotted with holes. What the hell kind of magic had I just thrown at her?

Jude rushed to Lavender's side and dropped to her knees by the girl.

Is she okay?

I wanted to speak the words out loud, but it was super obvious that no one wanted to hear from me. Half the other students looked at Lavender, concern on their faces. The other half glared at me.

Jude looked up, then pointed a finger at me. "You and I need to talk. Later."

I nodded. "Yep."

Jude turned back to Lavender, who was trying to sit up, but failing.

A low meow caught my ear, and I turned.

Muffin sat in the doorway, his skinny, hairless body as dark as shadow. His green eyes gleamed, complementing the ruby in his tattered ear. Frazzled whiskers twitched. Behind him, Bojangles rolled by, chasing his orange tail.

Come on, failed hunter.

I glanced back at Jude and the rest of the group, torn. Did I stay here and wait for my talk? Or find out what Muffin wanted?

Since I didn't like getting yelled at, it was an easy choice.

I hurried toward Muffin on silent feet, slipping from the training room. Lachlan waited out in the stone-walled hallway, a fluffy Princess Snowflake III draped over his shoulders.

"I have no idea how she got up here." He pointed to the cat, bemused. "One second she was on the ground, then she was here."

She rubbed her face against his, white fur sticking to the dark stubble on his cheeks.

"Hey, Princess," I said.

She turned to me, blue eyes glinting, and hissed.

"I love you, too." I grinned. "Don't forget that dead mouse painting you made me. Maybe you did it in a moment of weakness, but I know you like me."

"Dead mouse painting?" Lachlan asked.

"Yeah, I'll show you sometime." I looked back at the door. "Let's get out of here. Did you find Torlock?"

If he had found a good clue, I could bring that to Jude. Maybe it would smooth over the hair-loss incident with Lavender. Not that Lavender would ever forgive me—that was a lost cause. But I needed to get on Jude's good side.

"Yes, I found her. She's hiding in a realm of shadows and mystery."

"Of course she is. What's it like?"

"It's a place that takes myths and fairy tales and twists them."

I frowned. "Is there a difference?"

"I'm not sure. But it's going to be dangerous. You need contacts and an invitation to find her. We have neither."

"But we have our wits."

He smiled at me. "That we do. And also some moderately reliable directions."

"Moderately reliable? I can deal with that." Then I frowned. Caro, Ali, and Haris were on the trail of this, too. If we were hunting something as big as this, shouldn't I give them a heads-up? We'd lose our lead—and I *really* wanted to be the one to bring this info—but this was bigger than me. Anyway, working as a team had helped us save Connor last week. It was always the smart way to go. "I think we should give the others a heads-up."

"Agreed. Are they here?"

"Maybe." I touched the comms charm at my throat. "Rowan? You here?"

Bree was off hunting that demon in Ireland, but Rowan should still be here. I'd called her when I'd gotten back earlier this morning, just to make sure she wasn't on lockdown.

"Hey! Yeah, I'm in the kitchen with Hans and some other folks."

"Caro, Ali, or Haris part of that gang?"

"You're in luck. They stopped by to pick up sandwiches to go from Hans. They're on the hunt for a clue."

"Good. We'll be there in a sec. I want to talk to them."

"I'll tell them to hang on."

Lachlan and I hurried through the hallway, heading toward Hans's kitchen on the bottom floor of the castle. Princess Snowflake III rode on his shoulders the whole way, and though he looked slightly uncomfortable and weirded out, he didn't boot her off.

It was a smart decision, since she might claw his eyes out. Muffin stalked alongside, while Bojangles rolled like a tumbleweed, chasing his tail.

"How does he not turn his brain to mush, doing that all the time?" I asked.

"Meow," Muffin said. *Everyone needs a hobby.*

"True."

We entered the main entryway and took the stairs down to the kitchen.

Hans took one look at us and shouted, "Juice!"

I caught the juice box that he hurled at me, and Lachlan did the same.

"Do I look that bad, Hans?" For whatever reason, the head cook at the castle was convinced that juice solved all ills.

Hans shrugged, mustache quivering. "You could always use juice."

I stuck the straw into the little box. "Thanks."

He nodded. Boris sat on top of his chef's hat, the little brown rat snacking on a piece of cheese. He eyed Princess Snowflake III, but didn't so much as twitch a whisker. Boris was a tough rat.

Caro, Ali, and Haris stood near the table, each with a brown paper sack in hand. Rowan sat with a big bowl of soup.

"Thanks for not turning my sister in," I said to them. Rowan had briefed me this morning, saying that Caro, Ali, and Haris had kept her appearance in the caverns a secret from Jude.

"No problem." Caro's platinum hair gleamed in the light, complementing her silver jacket and gray jeans. "But we can't do it often. Jude would kill us."

"Made a judgment call, though," Ali said, flashing a quick smile. "Rowan's good people."

She grinned. "Thanks, Ali."

"Why'd you want to see us?" Haris asked.

"I'm hunting for the same thing you are," I said.

"An extracurricular activity?" Caro grinned.

"Pretty much. But I didn't want to keep any info I found a secret, since I want to find Arach's magic."

"More than you want credit, you mean." Ali bit into an apple, his white teeth gleaming.

"Credit won't do me much good if we lose our friends and the Protectorate loses its magic."

"True." Caro nodded. "So spill."

I told her about the potion and Torlock, along with our plan to hunt her.

Caro nodded, clever eyes keen. "Good, I like the direction you're going. We're headed a similar way, but we're after another potion maker."

"Melevakan?" Lachlan asked.

"The very same," Haris said.

"Who's that?" I asked.

"The only other potion maker besides Torlock who could make the Sylthian Potion. We were going to find him if it didn't pan out with Torlock."

"We'll take care of Melevakan," Caro said. "You try Torlock. One of us will be right." Her gaze turned to me. "But don't tell Jude what you're doing. I think it's great, but she'll be uber mad."

"I don't want that." Still, I didn't consider quitting this. Not when we were on the trail of something.

"No, you don't. So we'll find some info, and if you're successful, then we'll tell her. If you fail, we'll pretend it never happened."

"Thanks, Caro. You rock."

I hadn't known her long, only a few months. Same for Ali and Haris. But they were awesome. Rowan caught my eye and grinned. I knew she was thinking the same thing that I was—it was good to have friends. We hadn't had many in our lives, but I could get used to it.

Ali frowned. "But she'll find out, you know. Jude sees all. So you'd better find something."

"And it better be good," Haris added.

Caro scowled at them. "I can always count on you guys to be buzzkills."

"But we're right, aren't we?" Ali asked.

"You are." Caro turned to me. "I hope you find something big. Big enough to make Jude forget she's pissed that you broke the rules."

I swallowed hard and nodded. "Roger."

We grabbed a couple sandwiches, then wished the other team good luck.

"Be careful," Rowan said.

"I promise." I hugged her, then followed Lachlan from the room.

We hurried up the stairs and through the main entry hall, then out to the courtyard.

I turned to Lachlan. "So, where is this land of fairy tales and myths?"

"Bavaria."

"Of course it is." I didn't know where exactly the Brothers Grimm were from, but it was somewhere in Germany.

Lachlan raised his hand, his magic swelling on the air. Sneakily—or at least, I hoped I was sneaky—I sucked in a whiff of his intoxicating forest and leather scent.

Then the portal appeared, and I stepped through. The ether sucked me in and spun me around, then spat me out at the edge of a forest. Though the sun was high in the sky, it was shadowed here. The trees were as gnarled and ancient as those in the Enchanted Forest at the Protectorate, but somehow much, much darker. There were no fairy lights floating between the trees, for one.

Lachlan appeared next to me, nearly bowling me over.

"Sorry." I stepped aside, realizing that I'd forgotten to get out of the way of the portal exit. "The forest just…"

"Distracted you?" Lachlan studied the trees that were about ten feet away from us, but somehow, it felt like miles. "I can see why."

"What is it about this place?" I sniffed the air, trying to get a sense for the type of magic that surrounded me.

All I caught was the rich scent of dirt and the fresh scent of leaves. The air was completely still, though, with an eerie quality that suggested we were being watched.

"I have no idea." Lachlan stepped toward the trees. "It's a strange magic, though."

"No kidding. Which way do we go?"

"We head east through the forest, to start."

"All right, then." I shivered as I followed him, inspecting the twisting trunks and branches of the little trees. The bark was pitch-black, and the leaves a dark green. White specs nestled within the leaves, and I squinted upward at them.

We were about a dozen feet inside the forest when I realized what the white specs were.

'They're eyes." A chill raced over my skin.

Lachlan just grinned.

I kept my gaze on the eyes that followed us. The air was unnaturally still, as if we were sealed in some kind of fancy space chamber. Leaves crunched underfoot, and the eyes seemed to glare.

I drew a dagger from the ether. Just in case.

"Nervous?" Lachlan asked.

"Smart."

"Aye, you're that."

A little gray rabbit peeked out from beneath a bush. It wore a tiny top hat perched jauntily over its long ears.

"And who might you be?" I asked, charmed.

The rabbit bared its teeth, which turned out to be long fangs that dripped blood.

I cringed back. "All right, all right."

"Let's keep moving," Lachlan said.

I skirted around the rabbit quickly. "What, you're afraid of a bunny?"

"You bet your arse I'm afraid of *that* bunny. He can probably clean a corpse in minutes."

"He eats the dead?"

"Well, I assume he eats them *once* they're dead. Whether or not he makes them dead, I have no idea."

"This place is officially nuts."

"I think that devil rabbit is going to be the least of it."

We walked in silence for nearly an hour, our senses ever alert. The Cats of Catastrophe appeared out of the blue, somehow having made their way to us. I almost asked Muffin, but it seemed like he could read my mind when he shot me a look that clearly said, *Magic, dummy.*

The Cat Sìth had a lot of tricks up his sleeve.

He and Princess Snowflake III stalked quietly through the leaves, their movements lithe and graceful despite Princess's bulk and Muffin's little belly.

Bojangles, on the other hand, was the opposite of stealth. He bounced off the tree trunks like a bouncy ball on steroids, keeping himself entertained as he followed along.

"How do you rob banks with that guy blowing your cover?" I asked.

Muffin looked at me. *Bojangles has skills you can't even imagine.*

I stifled a laugh, barely holding it in.

Muffin gave me a look that was entirely unimpressed. *You'll see. If you're lucky.*

I nodded, not wanting to piss off my sidekick. But I *definitely* didn't tell him he was my sidekick. That would get my butt kicked. By Princess Snowflake III, if not by him. She wouldn't even be a sidekick by association.

As we walked, snow began to appear on the ground. Weirdly, it wasn't falling from the sky, and nothing else about our surroundings changed except for the air growing colder. It was the fastest regional temperature change I'd ever experienced.

The snow became thicker quickly, until I was crunching on top of the semi-frozen crust. Bojangles ran and slid along the top of it, sending it spraying, while Princess Snowflake III minced her way through it. Muffin just plowed forward, head low and determined.

I looked down to check his hairless body, sure to see him shivering, and realized that he was wearing little boots.

"Where'd you get those?" I asked.

Always be prepared. I was a Cat Scout.

"Really?"

Oh, you sweet summer child.

"So, there are no Cat Scouts?"

He just shook his head like I was a moron.

I scowled at him, and he grinned toothily back at me.

Then a drop of red blood landed on the snow in front of his paws. It spread outward, red and bright. He stopped abruptly, back arched, and I stepped back. Dark magic rose on the air, prickly and sharp.

"What the hell—"

5

The red spot grew outward, quickly snaking through the white snow. Then it rose up, forming the shape of a man. He was built of bloody snow, and he lunged for me, so quickly that I didn't have a moment to react. His icy body plowed into mine, and I crashed onto the cold ground.

His freezing hands reached for my throat and grasped it, his touch slippery and icy.

I kicked up at his belly, blasting a hole through the snow. But his hands remained, tightening around my throat as my vision blackened.

Muffin lunged for his hands, his little body plowing through the snow that clutched my neck and scattering it.

Gasping, I sat up.

All around, drops of blood fell from the sky, landing on the white ground. Bloody ice men popped up from each drop and lunged for us. Lachlan was already fighting four, his blade cutting through their middles. They tumbled to the ground, but crawled toward him like zombies, their hands dragging their torsos along. He took out two ice men, then raised his hand.

As his magic swelled on the air, I drew my sword from the

ether and lunged for one of the red ice men. His features were rough, but clearly human. Since kill shots weren't an option— blasting apart their snowy forms was the only way to go—I went for the waist, cutting him in half. They were easier to outrun in that form.

There were dozens of them, though, and I thanked fates for my sidekicks.

The Cats of Catastrophe shrieked as they launched their attacks, flying through the air to plow through the bodies of the ice men. As usual, Princess Snowflake III was covered in blood in seconds, her white fur stained red. Bojangles went after them with the fury of a thousand enraged kittens. He was as awkward as ever, but since this attack was all about brute force, it worked in his favor. He was a whirlwind. Muffin was efficient and quick, claws flying as he leapt from ice man to ice man.

I sliced through the waist of another attacker as the scent of Lachlan's magic made it smell like Christmas in the forest. The pine scent surged as a glint of silver caught my eye. He was calling on a nearby river, forcing the water into the air. It shot like a jet through the trees, aiming for the ice men. It plowed through one, obliterating it, before heading to another.

I kept an eye on the water as I fought. It plowed through the beasts faster than we could, but there were still so many. I took out one, then spun, kicking another in the chest and sending him flying backward. Red snow flew through the air as his body scattered.

A snowy attacker got me by the arm, squeezing tight. Pain flared, followed by icy cold. I swung my blade, slicing through his arm. The hand stayed clutched around my bicep, continuing to tighten. I kicked at the now one-armed attacker, sending him backward, and rubbed harshly at the snowy hand still attached to me. It crumbled away.

"This is some miserable freaking magic," I shouted.

"It's under control." Lachlan sliced his blade through an ice man, his other hand raised to manipulate the water that zipped through the forest, taking out our attackers. It avoided the cats, who were flying through ice men like feline trapeze artists.

My muscles ached as I fought, swinging my sword as quickly as I could.

Finally—freaking finally—we took out the last ice man.

The snow around us was coated with red. The dark magic that had pricked on the air faded, and I turned to Lachlan, panting. "That was close."

"What the hell were these beasts?" He rubbed watery blood off his face.

I dragged my shirt up to rub at my own face, wincing as the cold hit my belly. "I don't know, but it's some strong magic. Did your moderately reliable directions not warn you about this?"

He shook his head. "No specifics. Just keep heading east from the edge of the forest. And we might meet some helpful individuals along the way."

"So, just like a fairy tale."

He pointed to the bloody snow around us. "A screwed up fairytale."

"True."

The Cats of Catastrophe were frantically cleaning the blood off themselves, though Princess Snowflake III didn't seem to be in much of a hurry. She was the prettiest of them all, with her long white fur and elegant bearing, but she sure didn't mind a bloody tussle once in a while. Or every day.

Lachlan met my eyes, respect glinting in his dark gaze. "You fight well."

"Thanks."

He nodded.

"Let's keep moving." My body ached like mad, and I didn't

want these bloody ice men to wake up and start fighting again. Not to mention my chilly skin, which was starting to feel numb.

We hiked quickly through the forest, the cats at our side. It was quiet now that the battle was over, pristine and white. Frankly, it looked like a Christmas card. The glittery kind that I'd always admired, except that we'd never had anyone to send them to.

As we walked, the sense of danger left the air. No way that would last, but for now, it gave me a moment to catch my breath.

"When I met you outside your class, you seemed off," Lachlan said.

Apparently, he'd already caught his breath. And decided to use it to make probing and insightful observations.

I shot him a look out of the corner of my eye, annoyed and touched at the same time. "Why do you say that?"

"I don't know. You just had a look about you."

"Class didn't go well. Lavender kicked my ass, then I got pissed and whooped hers. With some kind of crazy light magic that I couldn't control. When I left, she was laid out on the floor."

"Was she all right?"

"Of course." *I think.* "She seemed all right. Mostly. And Jude seemed pissed."

"She wants you to get a handle on your magic."

"Duh. It went easier for my sister Bree. She's a total badass. I think Jude expects me to move as fast as her." And damn it, I wanted to. I was willing to do whatever it took.

He hiked his thumb over his shoulder. "I saw you back there. You were badass."

"Thanks. But that wasn't magic. That was regular old sword fighting."

"Your magic is totally unheard of and manifests in a different way than most people's. That's why you're having trouble."

"Um, thanks." It was nice that he understood, but it wasn't an excuse for me. I'd used every moment I'd had, to practice, trying to call out the magic and make it obey my command. It hadn't worked.

"First chance we get, I'll help you," he said. "I have some tricks."

"Thanks."

At my side, Muffin meowed. *I bet he has some tricks.*

"Shhhh." I kicked a little flurry of snow at him, and he batted it away with his paw, giving me an unimpressed look.

"I'm sorry I couldn't help you earlier," Lachlan said.

"Catching the cloaked figure is more important."

"I'm not sure about that, but I did get the tracking potion up and running. Hopefully it'll have some answers soon."

From up ahead, the sound of voices filtered through the trees. The five of us stopped, frozen. I glanced at Lachlan, brows raised.

He tilted his head, clearly listening. But it was Muffin who spoke. The cat had better hearing. *There are seven. All of them freaking out about something.*

"Are they a threat?" I whispered.

Muffin scrunched up his face—which was already pretty wrinkled—in concentration.

Bojangles hurtled forward, loping through the trees toward the voices.

"Bojangles clearly doesn't think so," I whispered.

He likes everyone. Moron. Muffin shook his head, his earring glinting. *But they are maybe not a threat.*

"Let's check it out." I crept forward, keeping my steps silent on the snow. As we walked, the snow disappeared quickly.

The forest floor returned to normal, and the trees grew larger. They were more like healthy oaks now, rather than the twisted and stunted creepy things they had been. The voices came through much louder, and a clearing lay ahead.

I snuck behind a large tree and peered out, Lachlan at my side.

In the clearing, there were seven tiny men, all dressed in old-style clothes. They were wailing and arguing, pointing at something in the middle of the open space that I couldn't see.

Dwarves?

As in, the seven dwarves?

Holy fates.

Bojangles streaked past, a little orange blur. He plowed through the men, heading for something.

"What the hell?" Lachlan whispered.

The dwarves flipped out.

"A cat!" cried one.

"Help us!" shouted another.

Help?

"Cat! You must help us!" yelled a dwarf wearing a funny bowler hat decorated with twigs.

Bojangles just meowed. I could imagine him, looking up at them with his goofy grin. Who would ask Bojangles to help them?

Fairy tale creatures, that's who.

I'd always wanted a bunch of mice and birds to clean my house. What I'd gotten was some violent cats to kick demon ass at my side, so I figured it was a win.

But the dwarves sounded desperate.

"Let's find out what they need." I couldn't just leave them. I crept out from behind the tree.

Lachlan followed.

We approached quietly. When I caught sight of the glass coffin, I couldn't say I was surprised.

A beautiful dark-haired woman lay within. The glass top was open, revealing her clearly.

Snow White.

This was what Bojangles had been running toward. He sat on her still chest, peering down at her pale face.

"Hi," I said.

The dwarves turned, their eyes widening at the sight of me.

"Help us!" cried one. His cheeks were red and round, and he looked like a cheerful Christmas elf. Except for the tears in his eyes. That wasn't super cheerful.

"Something terrible has happened to her!" said another. "Surely, you can help!"

I looked at Lachlan, but it was Muffin who piped up. *I'm not kissing her.*

Bojangles meowed, then swiped his tongue across her lips. I winced, knowing where that mouth had been. Snow White didn't sit up. No surprise.

"We're not her true loves," Lachlan said. "Isn't that what wakes her?"

My mind raced, trying to remember the original version of the story. There were a few, but one had always stuck out in my mind. It had been my mother's favorite, because it was downright hilariously weird.

The dwarves wrung their hands as they looked at me.

"She was poisoned by an apple, right?" I asked.

"We found one by her, yes!"

"Hmmm." I looked at Lachlan. "There's a ridiculous version of this tale where the prince shows up right about now—when she's in the coffin and everything. He's kind of a creeper and falls in love with her and begs the dwarves to let him take her body back to the castle."

"Her *dead* body?"

I nodded, grimacing slightly. "Yeah."

"Okay. Then what?"

"He carries her off, but partway home, he drops the coffin and she falls out. The shock makes her spit out the apple, and she wakes up. Then he tells her he loves her, and they're going back to his place to get hitched and live with his mom."

Lachlan rubbed his face. "Fates, that's a bad story."

"No kidding." I started toward the coffin, determined to save Snow White from such a ridiculous fate.

Maybe she was meant to end up with the prince, but the least he could do was take her on a date and get to know her. While she was *alive*.

I stashed my sword in the ether and approached her. Up close, she looked pretty dead. Pale as snow—but that was her thing, right?

Bojangles had settled onto her chest and was purring.

"You like sitting on dead people?" I asked.

He shrugged, as if to say he liked sitting on anyone.

"All right, then, but you'd better move. I think Snow White has had a hard enough day and shouldn't wake up with tuna breath in her face."

He shot me a confused look, as if he couldn't understand how *anyone* wouldn't like tuna breath. But he leapt off her all the same, grumbling.

Bracing myself against the grossness of sticking my fingers into a dead person's mouth, I pried open her jaw.

"Be careful!" cried one of the dwarves.

"Watch out!" shouted another.

They gathered around the coffin, staring at me with wide eyes as I stuck my finger into Snow White's mouth. It was wet and cold. I gagged, but fished around for the chunk of apple. When my finger hit it, I grinned.

All the dwarves gasped, probably at my expression, their round faces lighting up.

I pulled the apple out of her mouth, and she gasped, sitting up and slapping me in the face.

"Crap!" I clutched my cheek and stumbled backward.

"How dare you!" Then her eyes widened. "Wait, who are you?"

"Um, Ana? I just saved your life." I shrugged. "But I can see how slapping me would be a good instinct, seeing as how I had my hand in your mouth."

Her eyes widened, and it was obvious that she was remembering everything that happened. "That miserable old witch!"

"Yeah, maybe don't take candy from strangers?" I said.

"An apple is not candy."

Clearly she did not get the reference, but that wasn't my problem, and we needed to be getting a move on.

I looked from her to the dwarves. "We're looking for a city in this realm where Torlock the Dark is hiding out."

"Haven't heard of Torlock." The dwarf who spoke was clearly Sleepy. He looked like he was about to pass out at any moment. "But there is a city heading east. Avoid the tall green grass."

"Thank you," Lachlan said.

"Good luck, Snow White and dwarves," I said. "Make smart choices."

Snow White tilted her head. "Don't take candy from strangers?"

"Exactly."

We turned and headed back through the clearing. Bojangles gave Snow White a longing look over his shoulder, then followed.

We'd just reached the trees when the sound of hoofbeats echoed in front of us.

"Twenty bucks that's Prince Charming," I said.

"Aren't you worried about ruining her fate with the prince? She was supposed to marry him."

"Trust me. No woman wants to wake up in a coffin, being carried through the forest by some strange dude."

He nodded. "I see your point."

A white stallion appeared between the trees, and a fair-haired man who looked like he should be vacationing in Nantucket and wearing boat shoes peered down at us.

"Who are you?" he demanded.

"None of your damned business, Prince Charming." I wasn't super fond of a dude who would barter with some grieving dwarves to get the dead body of a woman he had the hots for.

He drew his sword, his face scrunched up. "The impudence."

I laughed.

Lachlan stepped forward, his gaze on the prince's sword and his magic flaring. "I wouldn't do that."

The prince frowned, assessing Lachlan. "All right, wizard. I shall let you pass."

"Good of you." I smiled. "But how about a word of advice?"

"Advice?"

"Yep. You're going to meet a pretty lady in the clearing. Why don't you try asking her on a date? Take her to a coffee shop. Fairybucks, or whatever you call it here. Don't just drag her back to your castle right away, all right?"

"Fairybucks?" He frowned.

"Trust me, pal. Date first, castle dragging later. And only if she says yes *before* the dragging."

"All right." He spoke slowly, as if I were a crazy person that he was trying to diffuse.

I took it as a victory, and walked past him.

Lachlan chuckled as he joined me. "I think you did Snow White a favor."

"I hope so. Because Prince Charming is a weirdo."

We hiked quickly through the forest, continuing to head

east. The air warmed as we moved farther from the snowy realm of bloody ice men.

"If we just went through the realm of Snow White, how did the bloody ice men factor into that tale?" he asked.

I searched my memory for the version that my mother had told me. "Snow White's mom was sitting by her window, before she had Snow White. A drop of blood fell to the snow, and somehow that made the queen want a baby."

"Which became Snow White."

"Yep. Fairy tales are weird, man."

"That they are."

We kept hiking, following Bojangles as he darted through the trees, bouncing off the trunks, his orange fur glinting in the low light of the sun that inched ever closer to the horizon.

The trees became stranger as we walked. First, the bark smoothed out. Then the trunks became purple. Finally, the limbs became smooth and tapered, like octopus tentacles.

"This can't be good," I said.

As soon as I spoke, a loud vibrating noise filled the air. I glanced around, and the cats did the same. Muffin raced up a tree, perched on a tentacle-like branch. It began to whip around, but he dug in with his claws, crouching low over the limb as he inspected the sky.

Bugs coming.

"What do you mean, bugs?" I asked him.

I drew my sword from the ether, studying the space around us.

A dozen massive insects appeared through the trees. Flying cockroaches and bees and butterflies—they were all brilliantly colored and glittered with magic.

I feel like I'm on a trip! Muffin meowed. *Haven't felt like this since my kittenhood when I tried those magic mushrooms.*

Bojangles meowed.

Don't experiment, kids.

I laughed as I studied the giant bugs. Despite their wild and friendly coloring, these things were *not* going to be friendly, that was for danged sure.

An enormous bee was headed straight for me, ready to strike. Its stinger pointed my way, big enough to skewer me.

The magic that filled the air made me feel stoned. I'd never tried drugs—though apparently my cat had—but this *had* to be how it felt.

I lunged for the big pink and blue bee, pointing my sword right at it. "You're going to have to impale yourself, buddy!"

He eyed the blade and darted around, clearly trying to attack from behind. I circled, keeping an eye on his approach. Lachlan's magic filled the air, the scent of pine and the sound of rolling thunder. Something was coming.

But in the few seconds it took him to conjure his magic, we had about twenty giant insects headed right at us.

It was like staring down the barrel of a psychedelic gun.

Muffin leapt from his tree branch, landing on the back of a brown moth with massive fangs. He yowled as he attacked the insect's neck, and the moth whirled on the air, losing control.

Princess Snowflake III and Bojangles teamed up. The little orange cat crouched low, while Princess Snowflake III raced toward him and leapt onto his back. Bojangles heaved upward, throwing Snowflake into the sky. It was a weird choice, since she was the bigger cat, but she flew gracefully toward a giant wasp, her fangs aiming for the insect's throat. She grabbed on, wrapping her claws around him.

On the ground, Bojangles raced up a tree, clearly intending to get his own piece of the action.

The pink and blue bee lunged for me, so fast that it was nearly a blur. I stabbed at its stomach, making impact as it tried to pierce me with its stinger. I was too slow, and the pointed bit got me in the arm. Pain flared. Stuck on my sword, the bee thrashed, then exploded in a burst of purple glitter.

To the left, Lachlan had his hands raised, magic glowing brightly around him. His silver and black aura was bright as a giant dragonfly swooped down toward him. The bright red and yellow creature shot a blast of green slime from its hind end. Lachlan dodged, barely avoiding the hit, which slammed into a tree trunk. The trunk sizzled, the acid eating away at the smooth purple bark.

Lachlan scrambled to his feet, raising his hands once more. Magic blasted from him, and wind kicked up, sweeping through the forest. It made the purple tree limbs wave wildly as the wind bowled over the insects. They tumbled through the air, then slammed into branches and hit the ground. The wind was so strong that it uprooted several trees, sending them crashing through the forest.

I dived, lunging out of the way as a tree hurtled my way. Muffin leapt off the back of the moth, landing in a run. He sprinted away from the body of a giant blue hornet that rolled across the ground.

I scrambled to my feet, the wind whipping at my hair. The gusts were strongest higher in the air, but it was still pretty fierce near the ground.

Lachlan lowered his hands, and the wind died. The strong signature of his magic fizzled from the air. All around, the insects lay amongst scattered trees. They rolled on their backs, trying to right themselves, but they weren't a threat at the moment.

I sagged, my muscles weak. "Whoa."

"I don't use that often."

"I can see why." We'd only survived because the worst gusts were higher in the air. They'd torn out trees, for fate's sake.

"Let's go before these things manage to get up."

"I second that." I hurried through the forest at his side, the Cats of Catastrophe racing to join us.

Muffin meowed. *I wouldn't turn down a second go at that!*

"You are nuts."

The other cats meowed as if they agreed.

Crazies.

We jogged through the forest full of purple trees, determined to outrun the insects. When we came upon a field of green grass, I stumbled to a halt. The grass blades rose twenty feet in the air, forming a nearly impenetrable wall.

"This is what the dwarves told us to avoid," Lachlan said.

I looked left and right, spotting grass as far as the eye could see. Both directions looked identical.

"Fates." *Which way will let us continue east most quickly?* I asked the strange new power that sometimes gave me answers.

Left.

Hey, victory!

"Let's try left," I said.

It took us nearly an hour to skirt around the green grass. By the time we did, the sun had almost set.

About ten minutes later, giant flowers appeared. They speared toward the sky, each blossom the size of a small house. Massive blooms of red and orange and purple made me feel like an ant.

"We have to be in Alice's Wonderland," I said.

"You know your fairy tales."

"My mother liked them." And so I liked them. Had she lived, maybe I wouldn't have. But now, they were pretty much all I had of her.

"The dwarves didn't say anything about flowers, and we're running out of daylight."

"Let's cut through."

Bojangles had already started, leading us between the stalks that were as wide as we were. About twenty yards in, the back of my neck prickled. On instinct, I looked upward.

An enormous pansy was reaching down toward me, bent over at the stalk with its bloom right over my head. Before I could gasp, the petals had wrapped around the top half of my body and picked me up, hauling me into the air. The blood rushed to my head as my stomach lurched.

6

Other blooms picked up Lachlan and the Cats of Catastrophe, their petals acting like strange limbs. When the flower holding me straightened its stem, I was over twenty feet in the air, sitting right in the middle of the blossom. The breeze blew my hair back from my face as I gazed out over a field of enormous flowers.

We were *definitely* in Wonderland.

A tulip straightened, and Lachlan's head appeared at the edge. The Cats of Catastrophe each sat on a giant daisy, looking super pissed. I opened my mouth to shout at Lachlan, but the flower heaved me up in the air.

I flew, tumbling through the sky, as a scream tore from my throat. A pink rose caught me, and I flopped down into its huge petals. They were smooth as silk and smelled like heaven, but a moment later, I was flying through the air again.

I passed Lachlan, then Muffin. Princess Snowflake III was hissing up a storm, while Bojangles meowed with joy. It was alternately terrifying and amazing.

Then the flowers threw us faster and faster, and the landings became harder and harder. No matter how soft the flower petal, if you hit it while falling from forty feet, it hurt like hell.

"Freeze time!" I shouted at Lachlan.

"I'm try—"

His voice cut off. Panic surged through me, and I whipped around, finding him falling limply through the air. A giant sparrow fluttered near him, a mallet clutched in its claw.

Holy fates!

It'd knocked out Lachlan!

Muffin meowed. *I'm gonna get that bird!*

His little legs kicked in the air as the flowers tossed him around. Valiantly, he tried to reach the sparrow, but he had no control over the direction of his flight. I tumbled through the air, my panic rising. The sparrow flew for me, the mallet raised high. Dark delight glinted in the bird's eyes.

Princess Snowflake III yowled. She was close to the bird. It turned toward her, and she went for its face, luck sending her flying right toward him. She clung to him, hissing and scratching, but he shook her off. A red tulip caught her. In the distance, Lachlan's unconscious body lay limp as it was tossed from bloom to bloom. He must have been hit right in the head. The cats flew through the air, hissing and yowling.

The bird spun in the air, heading for me.

I tumbled and landed on a daisy that flung me upward almost immediately. I'd lost all sense of time and direction as panic flared within me. I had to stop them.

The bird dived for me, its heavy mallet ready.

Sweat chilled on my skin as I called on my magic, praying that *anything* would come to the surface. My shield, the light, the prophecy telling me what to do. *Anything.*

The bird neared, swinging the mallet for me. I curled in on myself, barely avoiding the blow, and the bird cawed. It spun, returning for me.

I ignored it—I had to. I needed to put every bit of focus toward the magic inside me. It was faint, like the glow of a lighthouse far away. Desperately, I reached for it.

Muffin meowed. *Hurry up, failed hunter!*

But I was too slow. The bird swung its mallet for me and nailed me in the stomach. The wind rushed out of me as agony shot through me.

I tumbled through the air as the bird flew off, swooping high into the sky. When I landed on a giant fluffy pink flower, it threw me right back up into the air. Helplessness made my skin itch.

I reached a peak, then fell, catching sight of the bird going straight for Muffin, his mallet raised.

The mallet was so big it could kill the little cat.

Fear and rage boiled up in me like lava. *I have to save him.* Magic followed, flowing hot and strong through my veins. It lit me up like a live wire, blasting out of me and lighting up the sky with a bright white light. It blinded me as I fell back onto a flower.

And lay still.

Blinking, I sat up.

What the heck?

All the flowers were still, frozen in space. The bird was frozen, too, its gray body resting on a large sunflower and its mallet gone. Light glowed around the flowers and the bird, pale and pure. I could feel it, like an extension of myself.

Holy crap, was that my magic?

It had to be, but I didn't know how to use it.

The Cats of Catastrophe stood shakily on their blooms. Bojangle's messy fur seemed to have straightened out and his goofy grin was gone. He'd been bopped so hard he'd turned into a regular cat, and he did not look happy about it.

I scrambled across the tops of the flowers, leaping from a daisy to a poppy to a rose.

Bojangles was closest, and I fell on my knees next to him. I grabbed his little head and shook gently. His mouth twitched, then turned up at the corners. The fur on top of his head stood straight up in its signature messy style. He relaxed.

Muffin and Princess Snowflake III inspected him, sniffing his head.

"You good?"

He meowed, and it didn't sound nearly as distressed, so I stood. I needed to find Lachlan. He was farther away, his limp body nearly falling off a purple pansy. I scrambled toward him, leaping from flower to flower.

I was nearly there when the white light brightened in front of me. A glowing figure appeared, amorphous and indistinct. The power that emanated from it almost sent me to my knees. I stumbled to a halt, gasping.

"You are slow, Ana Blackwood." The masculine voice was heavy with strength, but the words pissed me off.

"Who the heck are you?"

"I would think you'd know that."

"Well, I don't." I couldn't make out the figure's features, but I could sense its scowl.

"You must embrace the light of life, or you will collapse in on yourself and disappear into madness."

"Is that a threat?"

The figure shrugged. "You've known this was your fate. I suggest that you try harder."

"You—"

The figure disappeared, and I almost screamed with frustration. I shoved it away, though. No time for musing over godly figures when Lachlan was about to take a two-story tumble to the forest floor. Quickly, I raced over the last of the petals, jumping onto his flower.

My landing shook the stalk, and he nearly fell off the edge. I grabbed his arm and held tight, dragging him back onto the soft purple surface. My muscles strained with the effort—he was one seriously heavy dude.

When he was safely situated on the flower, I bent over him, worry tightening my chest. Blood coated his hair. The sparrow had landed a head shot.

Fates. My heart clutched and my skin chilled.

I shook him lightly. "Come on. You gotta wake up. I don't know how long I can hold these flowers off."

They were pulling at my magic, trying to break free of its spell. I tried to keep part of my mind on the light, forcing it to hold the flowers captive. Control them, somehow. I shook Lachlan again.

He groaned, then blinked his eyes open.

"Thank fates!"

"Don't shout," he groaned.

"Sorry. Can you move?"

"I think so. What happened?"

"A giant sparrow hit you over the head with a mallet."

"A sparrow?" His eyes sharpened. "I fight thousands of demons in my life, and it's a bloody bird that gets me?"

"It'll get you again if you can't get your big butt over the side of this flower and down to the ground. I can't carry you."

He nodded, brow creased, and raised himself up. He looked around, eyes widening. "Is this your magic?"

"Yep. No idea how, though."

"Well done. Let's get out of here."

The cats had already started to shimmy their way down the stalks, and Lachlan and I followed suit, each of us sliding down a different stem. My legs were shaky as I landed. The cats wobbled up to me.

Let's shake a tail and get out of here.

"Wiser words never said, Muffin." It was almost full dark

now, and we'd lost the light. I tugged a little compass out of my pocket. The beat-up thing was enchanted to have a few uses, but right now we needed it for its original purpose. It pointed east, and I started off that way.

"Aren't you prepared," Lachlan said.

"Plan A, B, and C won't get you far if you don't know how to get there." I tucked the compass away in my pocket and matched my pace to Lachlan's. He was slower now, the head wound clearly doing a number on him.

We departed the forest of flowers and entered a fantastical rock garden. Every shape and size dotted the land, but it was the giant cat-shaped rock that caught my eye. No sooner had I spotted it than it disappeared, leaving only a grin behind. That, too, faded eventually.

"That was quite the show," a voice to my left said.

I turned, catching sight of a grinning cat. He was yellow and brown, with long whiskers and cunning eyes.

"The Cheshire cat," I said.

"The one and only." He inclined his head, but the gesture was somewhat mocking. "And who are you? Someone *special*, I presume?"

His gaze traced over me as he licked his lips.

Danger. Something in me screamed it. This wasn't some normal cat, and his interest was unusual.

"Not special," I said. "Not special at all."

"Hmmm." The cat's figure shimmered, as if he were only partly there. "I don't think that's entirely true."

Muffin looked at me. *Don't tell him what you are.*

No kidding.

The Cheshire cat's gaze moved to Lachlan. "Do you know what she is?"

He glared at the cat.

"I could get you a good price for her." The cat grinned.

Lachlan frowned at the cat. "You must be joking."

"Oh no." The cat's magic swelled on the air. "I can offer you all the wishes of your heart."

I blinked. Suddenly, it was a lot easier to take the cat seriously.

It had to be his magic, which swirled around him like a pale purple smoke, twisting through the air toward Lachlan.

Uh-oh. Muffin arched his back and hissed.

The smoke twined around Lachlan, making his eyelids droop. A blissed-out expression crossed his face, and he swayed.

"What's happening?" I demanded. "Stop."

Muffin meowed. *It's his magic. He's famous for it. The bastard is impossible to resist.*

The Cheshire cat's magic pressed in on me, feeling like a cloying hug. The smoke wrapped around Lachlan. "What is it you desire, human? You can have it, if you give her to me. Anything at all."

Funny thing was, I *believed* the cat. He could make it happen. Whatever Lachlan wanted, it would be done.

"Just tie her up and leave her here," the cat purred, his eyes glinting with an evil light. "Then your greatest wish is yours."

Don't! I wanted to cry out, but I couldn't. It seemed like a pretty good deal, actually. Lachlan should really take him up on it. Anything his heart wanted.

Anything.

Lachlan stood firm, a grimace twisting his features.

"Do it." The words were dragged out of me, though I wasn't very surprised. Why wouldn't I advise him to do something that would give him his heart's desire? I wasn't a totally shit friend. "Do it."

"Listen to her," hissed the cat. "She wants you to."

Lachlan shook his head, but it looked like a monumental

effort. Desire flashed on his face, pure and bright. For a second, I wondered what it was that he wanted above all else.

"No," he bit out.

And I believed him.

Muffin screeched and lunged for the Cheshire cat, white claws flashing in the moonlight. He tried to swipe the other cat across the face, but the Cheshire cat disappeared.

The purple smoke that filled the air vanished, its magic fading too. It released me, and I sagged, gasping. The sudden desire to support Lachlan in giving me to the Cheshire cat vanished.

But the cat didn't. He reappeared on another rock.

Muffin launched himself at the cat, his own magic filling the air. The Cheshire cat hissed, back arched, then sat down and tried to look unaffected.

"All right, all right, Cat Sìth. I won't make bargains with your humans."

Muffin hissed. *See that you don't, or you'll regret it.*

The Cheshire cat shrugged. "You are seeking something in this forest, I presume?"

"We are," Lachlan said.

The cat turned to stone again, but still spoke. "I am certain you are not seeking what you should be seeking."

"What should we be seeking?" I asked, though I definitely didn't trust him.

"Shelter for the night. You are not from this forest, and the devil rabbits know. They will come for you soon."

"Those rabbits with fangs?" The memory made me shiver. If there were enough of them, we were screwed. This sounded like a warning I could trust.

"The very same. But I can direct you toward shelter that will protect you for the night. For a price."

"Not me," I said.

"No, your friend the Cat Sìth has made that *quite* clear." The cat's gaze flicked to Lachlan. "And it doesn't seem like your human friend will accommodate me, either. *Very* unusual."

Muffin hissed for good measure, and Bojangles joined him, arching his back and hopping backward. The effect wasn't quite as terrifying as the little orange cat probably thought it was, but I appreciated the effort. Princess Snowflake III cleaned her claws, her eyes glued to the Cheshire cat. *That* threat was clear.

"What do you want, then?" Lachlan asked.

His gaze moved from me to Muffin. "Nothing you have, human woman."

Muffin's green eyes glinted. *I'll handle this.*

He sauntered up to the Cheshire cat and meowed.

The Cheshire cat listened intently to Muffin, then nodded. They were bargaining, though I couldn't tell over what. As I listened, I began to pick up the sound of rustling in the forest. I turned, searching the darkness beyond. The sun had fully set now, and the forest was much less cheerful. Considering that the cheerful version of this place had nearly killed us, I didn't want to meet the creepy version.

Magic sparkled around my sphynx friend, then the stone at his ear disappeared. It appeared a moment later in the Cheshire cat's ear.

The now-bejeweled cat grinned his trademark smile, then pointed behind him. "That way. Five hundred yards. You'll find a cottage for the night. Don't leave until dawn. And I suggest you hurry."

"Thanks." I eyed him suspiciously, then departed the clearing with my friends.

"Do you believe him?" I asked Muffin.

He shrugged a bony shoulder. *It will be a cottage. But it may be utter shite.*

"We'll just have to find out." Lachlan pointed to the glowing eyes that were starting to appear through gaps in the bushes. More appeared every second. As soon as they had the numbers, they'd charge.

The five of us raced through the forest, as fast as we could stumble along. Given our injuries and our aches, it wasn't an impressive speed, but the sound of rustling forest leaves and the sight of glowing eyes kept us going.

When the house appeared in the distance, we all skidded to a stop.

"Bloody hell," Lachlan muttered.

I stared at the candy and gingerbread confection. "You have got to be kidding me."

I wouldn't be complaining if I saw a house made of tuna.

I glanced down at Muffin. "Do you know who is in there?"

Santa?

"This is not the North Pole."

Muffin shrugged.

"The witch who lives there tries to eat children, is that it?" Lachlan asked.

"You don't know your fairy tales very well, do you?"

"Once upon a time, I did."

I grinned. "Once upon a time?"

"Seemed appropriate. But I started training early, so it's been a while since I heard a fairy tale."

Training in his magic, I had to assume. "Yes, the witch eats children. Hansel and Gretel are the most famous."

He eyed the cottage. "Let's go rescue them, then."

7

H e was right. Every muscle I had felt like jello, but I was going to have to find some strength. Because we had to save those kids, if they were in there. We were doing a lot of saving here in the fairytale forest, it seemed. Maybe the Cheshire cat had sent us here to save them. More likely, he'd sent us here to become dinner.

Quietly, we crept toward the house. My skin chilled as we neared, thinking of the old witch who would actually *eat* children. It had been a cute fairy tale when I was a kid. Now that I was actually going to *face* her? It was like meeting freaking Hannibal Lecter.

We crouched beneath the windowsill, then popped up and peered through the cloudy glass. It was sugar, if I remembered the tale correctly.

There was no one inside.

Dang.

A rustling sound from behind caught my ear. Witch!

I turned around to find her, but caught sight of dozens of fanged rabbits hopping toward us. They wore all different sorts of hats, and their eyes gleamed with evil light.

Oh crap!

"Inside!" I hissed. "Gotta get inside! Deal with the witch in there!"

We rushed in through the door, Lachlan leading the way. The cats scampered in, fur sticking out in all directions. Except Muffin, who just looked a bit shaky.

I stopped dead in the middle of the room, spotting two children with bags over their shoulders. One was skinny and one was plump, and both looked happy and tired at the same time.

"We're here to save you," I said.

"Too late, lady," Hansel said, flicking his blond hair back. "My sister took care of the witch."

"Burned her up real good." Gretel pointed to the oven behind her. The iron door was shut.

I swayed a bit on my feet at the idea of a body in there. "Well done."

"We'll be off, then," Hansel said. "Take care not to leave the cottage at night."

"What about you?" Lachlan asked. "There are hundreds of devil rabbits out there."

"They're called *Fangbunnies*." Gretel stressed the word like Lachlan was a moron. "And we're from here, so they'll leave us alone. They only eat visitors. So stay inside."

"With the witch?" I asked.

"She's dead." Hansel's tone was no-nonsense. A real *get-over-yourself,* fairy-tale style.

"Right. Of course." I nodded, pretending to be as tough as these kids. They were hardened little cherubs. "The rabbits are worse."

"You have no idea, lady." Gretel grinned. "Have a good night."

With that, they turned and walked out into the night.

I went to the window and watched them stride off, the

rabbits clearing a path for them, then I turned back to Lachlan. "Well, that was something."

"Those kids didn't need saving."

"No, they didn't." I pointed to the open and empty chests in the corner of the cottage. "And they cleaned the old witch out. Took every pearl and piece of gold she had."

"At least we don't have to worry about them." He went to the makeshift kitchen, which was made up of a table and chairs, along with some bowls and a pitcher. An ice box sat on the floor, and he opened it. "How do you feel about cheese and bread for dinner?"

"Better than I feel about eating her creepy house made of cake." And I was grateful that the options were vegetarian, given what she'd intended to do with the children.

The Cats of Catastrophe began to gnaw on the walls of the house, seeming to enjoy the gingerbread. Bojangles got all the way into the rafters and started chewing.

"Careful, or you'll bring the roof down," I said.

He just kept chomping away.

I joined Lachlan in the kitchen and got to work tearing a piece of bread into smaller, bite-sized pieces. We sat down with our feast—including an old bottle of wine we found under the table—and stared at each other.

"Well, this is weird," I said.

He glanced over his shoulder at the oven, which was still warm. "Easily the creepiest meal I've ever eaten."

We ate in silence for a short while, satisfying the worst of our hunger.

"If those devil bunnies weren't waiting for us, I'd be out of here so fast it'd be like I disappeared into thin air." I took a bite of the bread and cheese, grateful that it tasted normal. "But since there *are* devil bunnies out there, I'm going to enjoy this stolen cheese and thank Hansel and Gretel for taking care of the witch. After today, I need a break."

"Aye." He touched his head, wincing. "I agree."

"How are you?" Worry tugged at me.

"Fine. Brain feels a bit rattled, but fine. I didn't even see the sparrow coming."

"He was a quick one. Why don't you take some healing potion? You brought some, right?"

"Aye." He nodded. "But we should save it. I'm not that bad off."

"If you're sure." I thought he was nuts, but he had a point. Who knew what was coming at us?

Lachlan finished the bread and cheese on his plate and sat back with his glass of wine. I avoided looking at his lips as he drank. Well, at least I tried to.

"Your magic," he said. "Tell me about the problems you're having."

I hesitated, wanting his help, but not really wanting to share the nitty-gritty of my issues. But how was he supposed to help me if I couldn't tell him what was wrong with me?

"I'll keep your secrets." Lachlan's voice was serious.

Trust. My instincts screamed it. I could trust him. He hadn't sold me to the Cheshire cat, despite the strong pull of magic that had made *me* suggest he do it. Hell, *I'd* almost sold myself to the Cheshire cat.

I chewed on my lip, debating. "Fine. I have new magic that is starting to appear, and I can't control it. I can feel it inside, and it sometimes appears when I need it. But other times it lays dormant."

"*New* magic is appearing?" Interest flared in his gaze.

"Yeah." That was the unusual part—one of the parts I'd been afraid to tell him. That almost *never* happened to super-naturals.

"And you're only having trouble with the new magic?" he asked. "What about the gift you were born with?"

"That has been acting up, too."

He leaned back in his chair and nodded. "All right. I think maybe I can help. I was born with different magic gifts, but not all developed at the same time. They lay dormant within me until I was older."

"How'd you get them to, uh...blossom?" The word sounded dumb, but it fit.

"A lot of trial and error, but what I found worked the best was focusing on *why* I wanted to use that magic. Desire could often jump-start it."

I nodded, thinking back. "Oooh, I think I get it. Back when we were being tossed around by the flowers, my magic burst out of me when the sparrow went for Muffin. His mallet would have killed him."

"Desire equals action."

"You didn't act on your desire and give me to the Cheshire cat."

"I'm not a monster."

"No, I don't think you are. But *I* almost sold myself away. How did you resist?"

"It wasn't hard."

"But what did you want when the cat said he could give you anything?"

Shutters closed over his eyes. "Another time, maybe."

I nodded, feeling my cheeks heat. That question had been the emotional equivalent of laying a kiss smack on his lips, and we'd already decided that was *no-go* territory.

"But you can't always rely on feeling a burst of strong desire to jump-start your magic," Lachlan said.

"No kidding. What do you do?"

"Now, I don't need any help. But when I was a child, my

parents sent me to apprentice with a great wizard. He used his own magic to help me access mine. Like a battery that could jump-start my own ability. I can try to do that for you."

"What would it involve?"

He stood and pushed his chair back under the table, then gestured me to follow him to the middle of the room.

I did as he asked, standing in front of him. The Cats of Catastrophe were curled up in front of the still warm oven, basking in the warmth of baking witch. Princess had a smile on her face.

I shuddered and turned to face Lachlan.

He raised his hand. "I'm going to touch your shoulders. Then I'll feed some magic into you. While I'm doing that, you choose a power to try to use. Really focus on it. How do you normally try to find it?"

"Most times, it's like a very faint light within me, but it feels miles away."

"All right. I'll try to help it glow brighter."

"You can feel my magic?"

"Some of it. One of my gifts is empathy. It's not my strongest power, but I can sense emotion and other people's magic. It'll help."

I swallowed hard, suddenly nervous. "All right. Let's do this thing."

I didn't really have a choice, after all. My haywire magic was starting to cause some serious problems. I still hadn't even faced the music for blowing Lavender off her feet and knocking her out.

Lachlan laid his hands on my shoulders, gripping very gently. His touch was warm and strong. A shiver raced through me, but I tried to suppress it. I dragged my attention away from the heat of his palms and closed my eyes, unable to look up at him, standing so close. I didn't trust myself not to lean up and kiss him. His scent twined around me, the smell of an evergreen forest combined with his skin making me sway slightly.

I shook myself, trying to concentrate on the magic within me.

"Which gift are you reaching for?" His voice was slightly rough, as if he, too, was affected by our closeness.

"The weird light that repelled the sickness wraiths and stopped the flowers from attacking us. I have no idea what it's called or what it really does, but it seems easier than the prophecy power."

"Sounds like it's related to life," he said. "If it drove back sickness and controlled plants."

"Maybe." I drew in a steady breath and focused on the magic within me. It was like an amorphous cloud, filling me with a sense of completeness. A sense of power.

But it was unformed. Unorganized.

"Try to visualize," Lachlan said. "That can help."

I nodded, imagining that a fog filled my body. Within it, the lights of my different powers glowed. They were faint, but I could see them.

I zeroed in on the pale white light that I was trying to master. It sat low in my belly, waiting to be called to the surface.

As if he'd sensed me focusing in on it, Lachlan fed his magic into me. His hands burned as it flowed through my shoulders and into my body.

I gasped, stiffening.

My head swam.

We felt *connected.*

His magic was strong and pure. I could feel the honor that flowed within him, the strength and conviction and goodness. And the heat.

He wanted me.

But he'd wrapped that desire up tight, getting a serious grip on it.

I squeezed my eyes shut and tore myself away from the connection with him. I didn't know if it was supposed to happen when he sent his power into me, but it was dangerous.

Instead, I reached for my magic, for the light in the bottom of my belly. It glowed brighter. Like a firefly that was really trying. Lachlan's magic was somehow grabbing onto my magic and feeding it.

I reached for the light, trying to grasp it with my consciousness. It was a weird, ephemeral action, but I could feel the light beginning to fill me.

I was doing it!

The little light that had glowed within my belly became brighter, burning away the fog that filled me and replacing it with a powerful glow that gave me a massive burst of energy.

It healed the aches and pains that rippled through my muscles, then filled me up with energy.

Lachlan gasped, a low, ragged sound that made my heart race.

My eyes popped open.

His face glowed, bathed in a pale white light.

It was coming from me.

"I think you've got it." His voice was husky.

Suddenly, I remembered how close we were standing. How I felt the desire within him.

I was barely a foot from him, so near that I could feel the heat radiating from his chest. Dark stubble coated his jaw, giving him a rakish look. The heat in his eyes completed the effect, and I swallowed hard.

His scent twined around me, intoxicating.

My heart thundered in my ears, and I swore I could feel

every molecule of air in my lungs. I could feel every molecule of *me*.

Particularly where his hands touched me.

My gaze dropped to his lips. So tempting.

No.

I couldn't.

He was fighting this, too. I couldn't be the one to break.

I stepped back, severing contact. It was one of the hardest things I'd ever done.

"How did I do?" I asked.

Lachlan dragged his gaze away from my lips, as if he, too, was just remembering the restrictions we'd placed on ourselves.

"Well, I think." He touched his head, a smile spreading across his face. "My head feels better. I think you have some kind of healing light."

"A healing light that I've somehow managed to weaponize." I'd always been sick of having defensive magic in an offensive world, so this was actually pretty cool. "I understand how I used it to drive away the sickness wraiths. Healing is the opposite of what they are, so they couldn't come near me. But the plants?"

"In a sense, healing is life. So you somehow used it to freeze them. Controlling their life forms."

The hair on my arms stood on end. "That's intense. If I could learn to do that with people..." I shuddered. "I really don't want that level of power."

"Right now, it's only manifesting as freezing plants and animals—and only those of your choice, because the Cats of Catastrophe weren't affected, correct?"

"True." I stepped back, needing to get a bit of space. "Let me try again without the help."

He nodded. The glow of my light had faded from his face, so I assumed I was starting with a blank slate.

I closed my eyes and focused inward, calling on the magic

within me. There was still the dark fog filling my body, but the white light glowed a little brighter. As if I'd made a pathway toward it with Lachlan's help, and now it was easier to find. I called upon it, reaching for it.

Seconds passed, then a minute. But slowly, it began to glow brighter, filling me up.

Euphoria seemed to fill me this time, as if the light weren't busy healing my wounds so it was able to give me a shot of pure happiness.

"Whoa." I opened my eyes and stumbled backward.

Lachlan grabbed my arms, keeping me from going down on my butt. The heat of his hands shot through me, and I glanced up at him.

Light glowed on his face again, and even more heat filled his eyes.

"Do you feel that?" I asked

He nodded, his gaze tracing over my face. I couldn't read what was in his eyes, but I could feel it.

And it was *hot.*

He shook his head as if coming out of a trance, and backed up. "You've done well."

I cleared my throat, dragging my thoughts away from kissing him. "Thanks. I still have a lot to work on, but I'm starting to feel a bit better about it."

"With practice, you'll learn what your gifts are capable of." His gaze sharpened on mine. "I think you're going to be very powerful, Ana Blackwood."

I thought of Bree, and the insane power that she was now able to wield. "I think you might be right."

The next morning, I woke with a sore back and an aching neck.

Rays of sunlight burned my eyes, and I groaned, sitting up off the hard floor. Why the hell was I sleeping on the floor?

Blearily, I blinked, spotting the three cats napping near the old oven, which was cool now. The whole house was cool.

The whole house was made of *gingerbread.*

Right. That's why I was sleeping on the floor. Because I had refused to sleep in the witch's bed. Lachlan had also refused, and he'd bunked down on the other side of the room. It'd taken me a while to fall asleep last night, mostly because of the thoughts of him that raced through my head.

But he was gone now.

"Hey, Muffin!"

The curled-up cat meowed loudly, a clear *What the heck?!*

"Sorry, pal. Did you see where Lachlan went?"

I was asleep.

"I know your ears are good enough to hear him leave even if you're asleep."

He inclined his head. *True. He left about thirty minute ago.*

I stood, rubbing my aching neck, and went to the window. There were no devil bunnies out there, thank fates. And the sun had risen, though it was very low in the sky. We couldn't be more than thirty minutes past sunrise.

I opened the door, the scent of dew on the grass greeting me. The air was chilly, but fresh, and the rolling green field stretched toward the trees in the distance.

"Hard to believe this place is full of devil rabbits and murderous pansies," I muttered.

Muffin meowed as he passed me, on his way to find a suitable bush, no doubt.

I stepped off the stoop, but before I could go far, Lachlan appeared around the side of the house.

He raised the basket in his hand. "I come bearing gifts."

"Food?"

"Food that wasn't in the witch's house, which makes it even better."

My stomach growled. "Excellent. What did you find?"

"Strawberries."

"Perfect."

As the cats chewed on the walls, devouring the gingerbread that was so oddly to their liking, Lachlan and I ate the strawberries and a bit of leftover bread and cheese.

When we were done, we left the cottage. The cats had eaten so much of the gingerbread base that it leaned slightly to the left.

"That won't stand for long," Lachlan said.

Bojangles burped, and the frosting on his lips quivered.

"Well done, cats," I said. "Now another creepy witch can't move in."

As if to punctuate my words, there was a great crash behind me. I turned. The cottage had collapsed in on itself.

I dusted my hands off. "Good riddance to bad rubbish, right?"

The cats meowed.

We continued heading east, following the rising sun. The forest that we walked through was the most normal-looking one that we'd been in so far, with average height oak trees and a soft underbrush beneath our feet.

"It's too easy," I muttered.

Lachlan nodded, his wary gaze searching the forest around us. "Aye."

We kept walking, our footsteps silent and senses on high alert. Even Bojangles kept the racket down, though it was weird to see him walking like a normal cat rather than bouncing around like a ball.

When the bushes ahead started rustling, I was almost relieved. Carefully, I drew my sword from the ether, keeping my gaze pinned on the foliage ahead. I poked around inside myself for my magic, making sure it was ready to use if I needed it.

It was. Sort of.

When the rabbit burst out of the bushes, I stopped.

He was about as tall as my waist, with bright white fur and a very fine brocade vest. The top hat on his head bore a decorative feather, and the monocle over his right eye was trained on us. A pocket watch was gripped in his little hand.

The White Rabbit from *Alice in Wonderland*.

"Are you late?" I asked.

"Not at the moment, no." His whiskers twitched as he inspected us. "Who are you? You're not from around here."

His question reminded me of the devil bunnies who devoured outsiders who dared trespass in their forest. I shook my head. "We're not. But you're not going to eat us, are you? We met some other rabbits who were obsessed with eating outsiders."

He blushed, his face turning pink all the way up to his ears.

"Do you know the devil bunnies?" I asked.

He blushed even brighter. Yep. The White Rabbit was embarrassed.

"You do," I said.

He cleared his throat. "I might have had a relationship with a vampire bat at one time, yes. But those children would not listen to reason!"

Holy fates, the White Rabbit was responsible for the devil bunnies because he'd hooked up with a vampire bat. I suppressed a laugh and shot a glance at Lachlan. His jaw was tight, as if he were about to burst out in a guffaw. Thank fates he held it in. It would definitely *not* go over well. The rabbit was far too uptight to appreciate us laughing at him.

Then the Cats of Catastrophe blew it. They started to laugh, a strange purring-meowing noise I'd never heard before. Muffin was on his back, skinny legs in the air.

The White Rabbit straightened, adjusting his monocle. "I hardly see what's so funny!"

Then he had no sense of humor. "I apologize for them. Terrible manners. Raised in a barn."

Princess Snowflake III hissed at me, and I was certain I'd pay for that remark later.

The White Rabbit glared, then swung his pocket watch around. It twirled in the air, magic radiating from it in white arcs of light. Two doors appeared behind the rabbit, one red and one blue. Both were large enough for Lachlan and me.

"You must select one to pass," the rabbit said.

"Where did this come from?" I asked.

His gaze darted to the cats, who were now sitting upright and panting. "It's the usual."

Somehow, I doubted that. The rabbit did not like being laughed at.

"What's behind either door?" Lachlan asked.

"I'm not telling *you*." The rabbit was aghast.

"Seemed like it was worth asking."

Flames burst up on either side of the doors, making it impossible to go around.

Perfect.

8

"Now pick a door!" The rabbit pointed.

I frowned. I really didn't want to go through the rabbit's doors. But I also didn't want to go through flame. I looked at Lachlan. "Any ideas?"

"None. They look the same. I'm partial to red, but that's a shite reason to go through a door."

"It is." I studied the doors. "Give me a moment."

I called on my magic, this time trying to access the strange premonition gift. It lay dormant within me, somewhere deep in my psyche. I closed my eyes, trying out Lachlan's trick of visualizing what I wanted. *Why* I wanted it.

Images of the Protectorate flashed in front of my eyes. Of becoming a full member and knowing I had a home where I was accepted. Where I was with my sisters. Of them being happy there. Because if I didn't make it in, they would leave with me. I didn't want to screw things up for them.

In my chest, the magic flared to life. It glowed with a blue light—or at least, I imagined it did—and made my mind feel clear and clean. Organized. Like a bunch of elves had come in and cleaned up all the shelves where I stored information, and I just had to ask my question and I would get an answer.

Which door do I choose?

Nothing.

I asked again. And again. Each time, trying to hold on to the light of knowledge that filled my mind.

Finally, there was an answer.

None.

The magic faded. I opened my eyes. "We're not going through either door."

"W-what?" the rabbit stuttered, stomping one of his big feet. "But that's...that's...."

"A good idea?" I walked toward the flaming wall to the left of the red door. "I know."

The cats trotted along next to me. I stopped in front of the flaming wall. Lachlan stopped at my side.

I looked up at him and grinned. "Trust me?"

He nodded. "Aye."

"Good." I held my hand up to the flame. Yep. As I'd expected, it wasn't hot. I stepped through, leaving the angry white rabbit behind. He was a wimp, though, if the story was correct. He wouldn't follow.

Lachlan did, of course. And so did the cats. I gave the wall of fire one last look, then started through the forest, continuing east.

"You used your gift of premonition?" he asked.

"I did. Using what you taught me. But I don't think it's premonition, exactly. It's almost like I know the answers I'm seeking. They come from within me, somewhere in my mind. Like I was born knowing. I just need to access it."

"You know everything in the world, then."

I laughed. "I don't think it's quite like that. But somehow I'm able to pull out some answers. Some kind of seer's gift, like my mother's?"

"Well, it's useful. I didn't want to end up wherever he was sending us."

"His house, I think. In the story, he mistook Alice for his housemaid."

"I don't think I'd make a good housemaid."

I chuckled. "I don't think so either."

We kept walking, cutting through the forest at a quick pace. I couldn't help but think back to how I'd managed to use my magic this time, calling upon it and actually having it *obey* me. Clearly there was something to Lachlan's technique.

I was getting better.

With practice, I might just get the hang of it.

"Any idea how far we need to go?" I asked.

"It's less than two days walk to the beanstalk. Then, we're almost there."

I stopped dead and looked at him. "Beanstalk?"

"We have to climb." He looked slightly guilty.

"You didn't tell me."

"Because you're afraid of heights." He shrugged. "Sorry. It seemed like a good idea at the time."

"To save me from worry."

"That was the idea. But I think we're close, now. There's not much worry-free time left."

Just the idea of climbing the mythical beanstalk up into the air made me break out in a cold sweat, so actually, I didn't mind that he'd hidden it from me. But it was a bad precedent.

I frowned. "Don't do it again. I appreciate it, but I can handle it."

He nodded. "Aye. Of that, I have no doubt."

Ten minutes later, a figure appeared between the trees. It

wore a long floral dress and a bonnet decorated with flowers. But the head that peeped out from underneath the bonnet was definitely no one's grandma.

"The big bad wolf." He walked upright, but was otherwise wolf shaped. I looked around for Red Riding Hood.

Muffin arched his back, hissing.

"Chill out, cat." The wolf stopped about ten feet from us, and Muffin settled down, as if he liked the vibe of this wolf. "What are you doing in these woods?"

"Passing through," Lachlan said.

"Almost no one comes here. Not on Thursdays, at least." He frowned, fingering his bonnet with a furry paw.

"Where's Grandma?" I asked.

"Playing bridge with the girls." An air of honesty rang in the wolf's voice.

"You didn't eat her?" I asked.

His face twisted, annoyed. "Red is still spreading tales, huh?"

I pointed at his outfit. "So, she's lying about you eating her grandmother and dressing up in Grandma's clothes in order to trick her and eat her, too?"

The wolf frowned. "First, I just like wearing Grandma's clothes, okay? I find it relaxing. And second, Red is a pain in the tail who just spreads stories."

"She doesn't like that you take her grandmother's clothes?" Lachlan asked.

"Rude!" The wolf pointed at Lachlan. "I don't *take*. Grandma and I have an arrangement. I keep the other wolves away. She lets me borrow her clothes. We're friends."

"Sounds like a good arrangement," I said. "And Red sounds like a jerk."

"She really is." He nodded, clearly pleased that I agreed. "So what's east? You're not going to Fairy Tale City, are you?" He gave us a skeptical look.

I glanced down at Muffin, who was looking approvingly at the wolf. Muffin shot me a look. *He's a good canine.*

Since I trusted Muffin's judgment, and the wolf wasn't setting off any of my alarm bells, I answered honestly. "Yes, we're looking for the beanstalk to get up there. We need to find Torlock the Dark."

"Hmmm." The wolf crossed his arms. His expression was even more doubtful. "You're going to need a guide."

"For what?" Lachlan asked. "The city?"

"And to find Torlock. Unless you have an invitation—which you don't, from the lily-white look of your auras—you won't be able to find her without a guide. And you'll get hassled in Fairy Tale City."

"What's white about our auras?" I asked. I'd seen Lachlan's. His was black and silver. Bree had said mine was green, though I'd never seen it myself. They didn't exactly show up in a mirror.

"I can see good and bad, dark and pure." He pointed at us. "And you two are pure. Like driven snow. You shouldn't be getting mixed up with the likes of Torlock the Dark."

"Not normally, no," I said. "But we need something from her. Would you be our guide?"

He nodded. "For a price."

"How much?" Lachlan asked.

"Not money." He pulled at his dress. "I've got everything I want. Friends, food, nice clothes from Grandma. But I do need a spot of help."

"With what?" I asked.

"That nasty Jack has been pestering the giant who lives on top of the beanstalk. He climbed up there and stole some gold. Then he stole the goose. Then the cow. Honestly, it's too much. And the dwarves heard him say that he isn't going to stop. He'll kill the giant if he has to, in order to get all his treasure."

"Jack sounds like a real piece of work," I said.

"An arse." Lachlan pulled no punches with his tone.

The wolf nodded in agreement. "Exactly. The giant is wealthy, but a little slow." He pointed to his head. "Marching around all the time. Fee Fi Fo Fum and all that. But he's our giant, and we're going to look out for him."

"And that's your favor?" I asked. "You want us to help you stop Jack?"

"Exactly." The wolf held out his hands. "Not kill him, mind you. I don't have the stomach for that. So far, he's just stolen. But we need to stop him, somehow."

"Do you have a prison? Or police?" I asked, imagining fairy-tale cops. Obviously, they were ferrets or something equally menacing but cute.

"No, we tend to do that at a local level." He pointed at himself. "Hence the wolf in a dress trying to stop a jerk from killing a giant."

I grinned. "Fair point. So you can't lock him up, and we can't cut down the beanstalk because it's how other fairytale creatures access Fairy Tale City, right?"

The wolf frowned. "You can see why this is a conundrum."

"Yep." I looked at Lachlan. "Any ideas?"

Lachlan thought for a moment, then patted his pocket. "Is there a lake nearby? One with a lot of weeds in it?"

"You're going to stop him with lake weeds?" the wolf asked him.

"Not exactly. But I'm good with potions. If I can find some Oblivisi weed, I can make something that will force Jack to forget the beanstalk and the giant. He'll walk by it and be unable to even see it."

The wolf grinned, revealing rows of sharp white teeth. "I like this plan. We'll go to the pond right away. You'll have a giant bullfrog to contend with, but if we can get past him, you'll get your weeds."

"The frog prince?" I asked.

"No. Just a giant bullfrog with a bad temper and a taste for wolf. Or any large animal, really. Including humans."

"Lead on, then," Lachlan said.

The wolf led us through the forest, his dress billowing in the wind. It was really quite flattering on him. I could see why he liked it. The cats seemed to have taken a liking to him, too—they seemed to like anyone who lived their truth—and walked alongside.

I smelled the fresh water before I saw it.

The wolf stopped and held up a furry paw. "We're nearly there." He pointed to Lachlan. "You, get your weeds. I'll be lookout. And you, lady, you distract the bullfrog. The cats could help. He might like them."

"How do I distract him?"

"A story might do it," the wolf said.

That didn't sound so bad.

"And if it doesn't work," the wolf continued, "try to get him to eat you, then lead him on a chase. He's pretty quick, but awkward. You should manage."

Aaaand, there it was. Nothing was ever easy. But I nodded. "Let's do this."

The wolf grinned again, extra fangy this time. He led us toward the pond, which gleamed with a dark light. Lily pads floated on the perimeter, but the center was empty. To the far right, a giant lump sat in the water.

The bullfrog.

"Be careful," Lachlan whispered, before heading off to the left.

The wolf gave me a thumbs-up. I smiled weakly, then walked right, mind racing with a story to tell the bullfrog. The cats followed alongside.

You got something good? Muffin asked.

"I don't know," I whispered.

Tell him about tuna fishes. They're very big and tasty. I could listen to stories about tuna fishes for hours.

"I'll consider it." If he thought about his stomach half as much as Muffin, maybe I could tell him tales of the giant bugs that had attacked us.

I neared the huge lump in the water. Fates, he was big. The size of the buggy, if not larger. His back and eyes were above the surface, while the rest of him was below. Could he eat me in one bite, or would it take two?

One.

I looked down at Muffin and whispered, "You're not making me feel any better."

I sure hope you have a good story.

In the distance, I spotted Lachlan. He was on the other side of the lake. He'd stripped off his shirt, shoes, and pants, and was clad in a tiny pair of tight shorts that I assumed he called underwear. I swallowed hard at the sight of his muscles, a broad expanse that would put Fabio to shame.

Eyes on the prize.

Startled, I looked at Muffin.

Princess Snowflake III meowed, and though I couldn't understand her the way I could understand Muffin, it was very clear that she was trying to say, *She is looking at the prize.*

The bullfrog shifted and snorted, blowing water up into the air. I stiffened, eyeing him warily. His big eyes popped open, and he stared right at me.

Showtime.

"Hi!" I jumped onto a rock behind me, trying to gain a little height and distance myself from the frog.

Like a mountain shifting, he rose out of the water. *Oh hell.* He could eat me *and* the cats in one bite.

"Who are you?" His voice was so deep that it vibrated through me. His enormous tongue snapped out, nearly touching my face.

I flinched backward.

Behind him, Lachlan eased into the water. As if he'd sensed the intrusion into his pond, the bullfrog started to turn.

"I'm Ana the Great!" I shouted. "Here to tell you a fabulous story."

The frog turned to look at me, interest suddenly gleaming in his eyes. "A story?"

"Yes. A great one." Did he not wonder why I had showed up out of the blue?

"Well, go on."

Apparently, not. The bullfrog wasn't the smartest. Considering that he could eat me, I was going to take whatever advantage I had.

"Well, one day, there were three girls." My mind raced, bringing back the tale of when my sisters and I had just started our business driving across Death Valley. "They lived in a very dangerous place called Death Valley. It was full of monsters of all varieties. Huge snakes and wicked birds with knives for feathers."

"Don't like birds," the bullfrog said. "Too crunchy."

I grimaced. Was I crunchy? Probably. "Anyway, the girls had a friend. Their only friend, in fact. He was an old man they called Uncle Joe, and one day, he didn't return from a trip across the valley. They knew that something terrible must have happened to him."

I peeked around the bullfrog, spotting Lachlan swimming out to the middle of the pond. Apparently, he was going to dive for the weed. Damn. That was dangerous. The bullfrog could definitely swim faster than him.

I started talking faster, hoping to entrance the bullfrog. "The girls set off on their first trip across the desert. They'd never done it before, and their vehicle wasn't nearly ready for the task. They didn't realize they were unprepared, but it wouldn't have stopped them."

"And then what?" the bullfrog demanded.

"Well, they—"

The bullfrog stiffened. "Intruder!"

How the heck had he figured it out? The bullfrog shifted, about to turn. Behind him, Lachlan was swimming back to shore, something green clutched in his fist.

Princess Snowflake III yowled, a shriek unlike any I'd ever heard.

The bullfrog whirled around, glaring at her with beady eyes. Rage flared within them. "*What* did you say?"

She yowled again. The bullfrog puffed up, clearly enraged.

Better run for it! Muffin turned tail and streaked through the forest. The other two followed, hightailing it out of there.

The bullfrog crouched low, clearly ready to leap after us in pursuit.

My stomach dropped.

Oh crap.

I turned and ran, vacating my rock just as the bullfrog landed on it. The bullfrog croaked. I sprinted as fast as I could, my lungs burning. The frog pursued, his giant leaps nearly landing him on top of me each time.

Muffin's weird, low meow sounded from the right, and I glanced over. He stood in a thicker patch of trees, in an area where the spaces between the oaks was much narrower.

Come on, slowpoke! Or you'll be frog chow!

I wheeled right and sprinted toward him. As fast as I could, I darted through the trees. Behind me, the bullfrog skidded to a stop. He was too wide to fit through the gaps between the trunks.

Princess Snowflake III yowled again, clearly unable to help herself from hurling insults at the frog.

"Come on, guys!" I spun and raced away, the cats at my side.

Behind us, the bullfrog croaked angrily.

That was fun! Muffin sprinted along beside me.

"You need new hobbies, if that was fun," I said.

He did his weird cat laugh. Up ahead, I spotted the wolf and Lachlan. The wolf held the green leaves, while Lachlan dressed again. I ran up to them and stumbled to a halt as my heart raced.

"Well done!" said the wolf. "That was clearly an excellent story."

"I didn't even finish. Did you get the Oblivisi weed?" I asked.

Lachlan nodded, his face flushed as he pulled on his clothes. "The weeds were thick at the bottom. It was easy."

"Good. What do you do now?" I asked.

Now fully clothed, he pulled a little glass vial from his pocket.

I recognized it. "Is that the healing potion?"

"Good thing I saved it, right? Same base properties as the Oblivisi potion. I just need to add the weeds." He took them from the wolf and made quick work of grinding them up with two rocks. Then he poured the dust into the open vial of healing potion. He held his hand over the vial, and his magic surged on the air. Sparkling light glittered around his fingers, flowing down into the vial. It smoked, giving off a foul scent, then he corked it. "All done."

"You have some kind of power over potions," I said. "That's one of your twelve?"

He nodded. "I can create things that others can't."

"No kidding." I shivered at the idea of a potion that could make you forget.

"What do we do with it?" the wolf asked.

Lachlan frowned. "That's the hard part. He must drink it."

The wolf laughed. "Oh, that's no problem at all. Give it here. I'll take care of it."

Lachlan handed over the potion. "How long will it take to find him?"

"With any luck, he'll be at his house. Come on." The wolf led us back through the forest. Fifteen minutes later, we neared the edge. The sun shined brighter through the trees, illuminating the little blue flowers on the ground. In the distance, a massive beanstalk rose out of the middle of a field. Huge rocks sat scattered around, as if a giant had thrown enormous marbles.

But it was the beanstalk that had my attention.

I swallowed hard, my skin chilling.

I was going to climb *up* that thing.

Holy fates, give me giant bullfrogs and devil bunnies any day. I looked at Lachlan.

As if he could read my thoughts, his face softened. "It'll be fine."

"I know. I'm tough."

"Look!" The wolf pointed to a figure crossing the field. It was a man wearing farmer's clothes, a straw hat shielding him from the sun. "That's Jack, headed to the beanstalk now. We were just in time. You two can follow, but hang back about twenty feet and stick behind the boulders. I need to talk to him."

He took off across the field, dress fluttering in the wind.

"This is so weird," I said.

"I quite like it," Lachlan said. "If you told me I'd be spending time with fairytale creatures and enjoying it, I might have said you were crazy. But as it turns out, it's not a bad time at all."

I grinned. He had a good point there. "Come on."

We hurried after the wolf, keeping the distance he'd requested and making sure there were giant rocks between us and Jack. When he stopped next to Jack, we stopped, too, hanging back twenty feet and tucking ourselves behind a huge boulder. I could just barely hear the wolf's voice. Jack's back was to us, so he couldn't see us.

Would this really work?

9

"Oy, Jack! How are you?"

I winced. The wolf was a terrible fake. His voice was too high-pitched and way stressed. At least I knew he was genuine when talking to us.

"Fine, wolf," Jack said. "Why are you acting so strange?"

"Oh, no reason." The wolf uncorked the vial and slowly raised it to his lips.

"What's that there?" His voice sounded greedy.

"Oh, this?" The wolf's voice cracked. "Nothing at all." He raised it to his lips again.

"Why don't you share a bit?" Jack asked.

"No!" The wolf jerked the vial back.

"Why are you being so selfish, wolf?"

The wolf wasn't the selfish one, that was for sure. And he might be a bad actor, but he was a damned good judge of character. Jack was a greedy bastard. No wonder he'd climbed the beanstalk so many times, endlessly stealing from the giant.

"Hey now!" the wolf yelped. His acting was getting a bit better.

Jack grabbed the vial and chugged it down, not seeming to realize that the wolf gave it up without a fight.

A moment passed.

Silence.

I glanced at Lachlan, who just smiled at me.

"Well, wolf, I think I'll be on my way. I must go help mother with the cow."

"Goodbye, Jack," the wolf said.

I peeked around the boulder, catching sight of Jack walking away from the beanstalk. "It worked."

"Of course it worked," Lachlan said.

We joined the wolf, who was picking up the vial and recorking it. He handed it back to Lachlan. "Well done, sir! That worked like a charm."

"And he'll never remember the beanstalk?" I asked.

"He won't. Can't even see it anymore."

"That's some powerful stuff." I eyed the vial nervously. He had the power to make people *forget* things. I'd been nervous when he'd made it, but seeing it put into use like that really made the hair on the back of my neck stand up.

"I'm careful how I use it. And Jack clearly deserved it."

True enough.

"Come on, then," the wolf said. "Let's head up the beanstalk. There's supposed to be a storm later, and you don't want to get caught halfway up in that."

Nerves skated along my skin at the memory of trying to climb the Eiffel Tower in the rain.

Lachlan reached for my hand and squeezed, sending a frisson of comfort and desire straight through me. It was a weird combo, but I liked it.

We followed the wolf toward the beanstalk. I walked quickly, locking my nerves up tight. *Focus on the job.*

We stopped at the edge of the beanstalk, which was much

skinnier than I expected. It was only a few feet thick, with knobby lumps and leaves sticking off it. I looked up, feeling my head spin at the sight of the stalk disappearing far up into the sky. It went on endlessly, swaying in the wind.

"I really wish you could make a portal," I muttered to Lachlan.

"Not to a magical realm I've never been to before," he said. "Sorry."

I sighed. "I've got this."

The wolf rubbed his hands together. "Right, then. Hold on tight to the stems of the leaves, and don't look up my dress."

I cracked a smile, and the wolf grinned at me. He gripped a couple of the leaf stems and began to climb. They looked sturdy enough.

The cats took one look at the beanstalk and shook their heads in unison.

We'll see you later. Muffin disappeared.

"Wimps," I muttered, though secretly, I thought they were pretty danged smart.

"You first," Lachlan said. "If you fall, I'll catch you."

I liked the idea, but... "I won't fall."

I'd gotten myself through worse stuff before, and I'd do it again. I gripped the leaves and hauled myself up. Hand over hand, I climbed the stalk. I didn't look up or down, just stared straight at the beanstalk and the next handhold.

"You're doing great," Lachlan said.

Though part of me bristled at the idea that I needed encouragement, I also liked the words.

As we climbed, the stalk waved in the breeze, swaying back and forth gently. It was attached to a cloud at the top, but that still left plenty of space in the middle for it to sway. My stomach pitched with every motion as I climbed, but I focused on the task at hand.

My muscles burned and my head spun, but I kept going. Hand over hand.

By the time I reached the clouds above, I was shaking. They were cool against my skin as I climbed through, finally reaching solid ground at the top. The wolf reached down and grabbed my arm, hauling me up behind him.

I scrambled onto the grass and collapsed, panting. I lay face down, cheek pressed against the soft green blades. I was learning to face my fears—heights—and master my magic.

Not bad.

By the time I stood, my muscles weren't shaking nearly so badly anymore. Lachlan looked bright and chipper, not winded at all.

"Are you all right?" he asked.

"Fine." I turned and inspected our surroundings. We stood in another enormous field. A huge castle sat in the distance. "The giant's place?"

"The very same. I'll tell him what you did for him." The wolf pointed in the opposite direction. "But we're headed that way. Fairy Tale City is only an hour's walk."

"As long as it's on flat ground," I said.

The wolf grinned. "You're in luck."

He led us across the grass.

We'd only gone a few steps when my comms charm blared to life. Lachlan and the wolf kept walking, giving me a bit of privacy.

"Um, Ana?" Rowan's voice sounded unsure.

"Yeah, what's up? Everything okay?"

"Um, yeah, well, you see—"

"Ana?" Jude's voice cut off Rowan's, as if she'd grabbed the comms charm. "What are you doing?"

Ooooh, fates. I was in trouble.

I swallowed hard, trying to sound casual and confident. "Following a lead."

Yeah, I did not sound that casual and confident. Even though I *was* certain this was the right thing to do.

"Judgment is everything. Orders are everything," Jude snapped. "I gave you an order *for a good reason.* And you disobeyed it."

"Jude, I really think we're onto something."

"It's not safe like this, Ana. You need to finish your training. Without it, missions are too dangerous. You need control of your magic, and you don't have it."

My cheeks heated. Not only had I run off, but I'd just blasted Lavender on her ass with my out-of-control power. I was zero for two lately on being a good member of the Academy.

"You know I can fight, Jude. That I can handle myself. And Lachlan has been helping me with my magic. I'm getting control of it."

"You'd better be, because the other department heads won't approve of this. Arach won't approve. It's too dangerous, and there are rules for a reason. We need to protect those who work for us, and we can't do that if you go running off untrained. It's because I care about you that I'm getting on you, and I don't want you to get kicked out of the Academy."

I swallowed hard. Hearing her say it made it real. And if that happened, my sisters would come with me.

I'd ruin their lives.

The Protectorate was the only place we wanted to be. We couldn't get kicked out.

"I understand, Jude. But we're going to find information that helps."

"For your sake, I hope so." She paused. "Be careful, Ana. Really."

"I will." But she was already gone.

Bree's voice popped in. "Ana?"

"Yeah, I'm here."

"Try to find something, okay? Because Caro, Ali, and Haris got back, and they struck out. You're our last hope."

Well, that felt like the weight of a semi-truck pressing down on me. "How's Florian and Arach?"

"Worse. They're fading more every hour. And so are the Pugs of Destruction."

My skin chilled. The pugs! "Oh no. That's…"

Shit.

We had to find answers.

"Take care of them, okay?" I asked. "I've got to go. We need to get a move on."

"Yeah. Good luck, okay?"

"Thanks." We were definitely going to need it, because failure was *not* an option.

I cut off the comms charm and hurried to catch up with Lachlan and the wolf, who were about forty feet ahead, waiting for me.

"Everything all right?" Lachlan asked.

"Not exactly." I told him about Florian, and the pugs, leaving out the part where I got yelled at and threatened with expulsion. That was bad enough without airing it to the world. "So we've really got to find answers."

"Aye, we do."

"Well, the town is just up there." The wolf pointed.

I squinted into the distance, catching sight of a low-hanging cloud. It was dark and ominous, crouching over the ground like a dragon.

"Let's go, then." I picked up the pace, nearly running.

We were about a hundred yards away when the wolf stopped near a cluster of large boulders. "Give me a moment."

I stopped next to Lachlan, my breath coming quickly.

The wolf stripped out of his bonnet and dress and stashed them in the crevice of the rock. At first, it was strange seeing him in only his fur. He wasn't *technically* naked, but after the clothes, it was a bit weird.

"Have to put on my game face." The wolf bared his fangs and growled.

"They don't like wolves who wear dresses in the city?" I asked.

"Oh, they don't mind. But it's hard to scare someone when you're wearing a bonnet, no matter who you are."

Yeah, I could see how that was true.

The wolf led us closer to the city, which seemed to be surrounded by the dark gray cloud. It hung low, turning the air cool and damp. As we neared, I realized that the city was built into a dark forest. Tall trees twisted toward the sky, with structures built between them and sometimes even *into* them. Purple and green smoke wafted from most chimneys, and the scent of dark magic rolled toward me.

I breathed shallowly, trying to avoid the stench of rotten eggs and old socks.

"You can see why I said you'd want a guide?" the wolf said. "It's not a nice place, this city."

"Clearly not. All the fairytale villains live here?" I asked.

"Most. And those that don't live here visit often." He straightened his shoulders, as if trying to make himself look bigger. "Stick close to me."

We stepped between the first two trees, entering the city at what was clearly a side street. The road was cobbled with dark stones, and two-story buildings ran along the left side of the street. On the right side, an enormous iron fence blocked off a huge estate.

"Is this the suburbs?" I asked.

"Fairytale style." The wolf pointed inside the fence. "The Queen of Hearts has a city home here."

My gaze traveled over the massive lawn that fronted the mansion. Heart-shaped bushes lined the drive, and the distinctive red roses sat in front of the house.

"Let's avoid her," I said. "I'm quite fond of my head."

"She's a nasty piece of work, all right," the wolf said.

We walked deeper into the city, moving past the mansions on the outskirts and reaching the more heavily populated area in the center, where larger buildings crouched between the trees. Most of the building fronts were dark gray, as if they'd been streaked with soot. I swiped my finger across a stone, wondering if it would wipe off.

"Dark magic," the wolf said.

He led us through the winding streets. They were largely empty, though I caught sight of people through glowing orange windows. It was so dark in here that it appeared to be night, the forest canopy shading the streets from the sun.

We passed an old wizard who sat on his stoop. He smoked a pipe that smelled like rotten weeds, and grinned toothlessly at us.

The next alley held a woman in a dark cloak. She clutched a shiny red apple and grinned evilly at me.

"Don't look at her," the wolf said. "You're pretty. She won't like you."

"Snow White's Queen?" I asked.

"Yes. She's always lurking about with that apple. Weirdo." The wolf shook his head. "We're nearly there."

I was damned glad I wasn't trying to navigate this myself, that was for sure. The city was huge, though it had an ancient feel. Dozens of winding streets, hundreds of buildings. It would have taken us ages.

A scuffle sounded from an alley up ahead, and when we

passed by, I caught sight of two large ferrets looming over a mouse wearing a leather jacket and a green scarf. In true fairy-tale style, they were all dressed in medieval-looking clothing and standing on their hind legs.

The ferrets were nearly as tall as I was, though the mouse was about normal size.

"Give us your gold or we'll eat you," growled one ferret.

"Well, that's not very original, now is it?" the mouse squeaked.

Oh boy. That mouse did *not* stand a chance against those ferrets. They were about forty times his size.

The ferret in the blue cap stepped forward, raising his claws.

"Hey!" I stepped into the alley. "Pick on someone your own size."

The ferret's beady gaze darted to mine. "Like you?"

Before I could respond, he hurled a blast of stinking magic at me. I dived left, drawing one of my daggers from the ether. I flung the dagger, but the ferret was fast, dodging right and avoiding my steel.

Lachlan's magic swelled on the air, and he diverted the water from a drain pipe right at the ferrets. It plowed into them, bowling them over. Their caps went flying as they crashed to the ground. They were only down for half a second before they leapt up and sprinted away, back down the alley in the opposite direction.

The little mouse turned to us and looked up. "You helped me, but you don't know me."

"Don't need to know you to help you." I rubbed my shoulder where I'd slammed into the wall.

"Hhmmm." The mouse grinned. "I guess you're right. I'll follow you."

"Okay." The least we could do was watch his back until we

got out of the city. Then he could return to his family in the forest, or wherever he lived.

The four of us trooped down the street, the little mouse faster than I'd expected him to be.

"What's your name?" I asked him.

"Robin," he squeaked.

"Like the bird?"

"Sort of."

"We're here." The wolf stopped by a dark green door. An acid green gem gleamed in the middle of the wood, and the windows glowed with a similar light. The whole place stank of burning tires and rotten fish.

I wrinkled my nose, desperate to get out of this stinky city and breathe some fresh air.

The wolf knocked loudly on the door. "Torlock the Dark! It's the wolf, here to buy some potions."

The gem on the door flared a bright blue, and I had to guess that it was some kind of magical peephole. A second later, a scratchy voice sounded. "Go away! You're not welcome here."

"Come on! I've been a good customer before!" the wolf said.

"Go away!"

The wolf frowned and looked at us. "I'm embarrassed to say that this was the only plan I had."

"Knocking on the door?" I asked.

He nodded. "I'm not much of a fighter. I can growl at people, and they usually don't bother me. But making the first move..."

"No problem," Lachlan said. "We'll figure something out."

"I've got this," the mouse squeaked.

I looked down. Way down. "You?"

He looked up and nodded. "Under control, milady. Just step back and let ol' Robin take care of the witch."

I stepped back, not wanting to offend the little mouse. When glittery green magic swirled around him and he grew five feet, I was damned glad I had.

The little mouse had become a giant mouse, with long fangs and even longer claws. The sword at his back was wickedly sharp. The green scarf at his neck wasn't a scarf at all. It was a hood peeking out of the back of his leather jacket.

Robin.

Hood.

"Hey, you're not just any mouse," I said. "You're Robin Hood."

The mouse grinned, his white fangs gleaming, and tilted his head. "The very same."

"No one ever said you were a mouse," I said.

"No one wants to admit to being robbed by a mouse," he countered. "And those I help keep my secret."

"You actually had the upper hand with the ferrets," Lachlan said.

"Most likely." Robin nodded. "But I appreciated the help. Now I'll return the favor."

He stepped up to the door and banged hard, sticking his eye right up against the green gem. "Witch! Open up!"

I shivered. His voice was downright intimidating. The squeak was long gone, and this was a mouse who took care of business.

"Go away!"

"You owe me, Torlock! Don't forget it." He gave a low growl. "And I always collect on my debts."

There was a shuffling sound, and a few curses, then the door swung open. A woman with a wild cloud of dark hair peered out, her black eyes gleaming brightly. The rest of her body seemed to be made of shadow. Her name was not ironic, then. She really was Torlock the Dark.

"Robin." She spit. "What do you want?"

"My friends want something from you." He turned. "I never asked what you wanted."

"Answers to some questions," Lachlan said.

Robin Hood grinned, and it was really quite charming. He turned back to Torlock. "Just questions. That's not so bad, is it?"

She scowled, her dark magic flaring. Unable to help myself, I pressed a hand to my nose and mouth to block the stench of old fish.

"Wiiiitch," Robin cajoled. "You know you want to answer the questions." He stroked his sword, and I'd never been so afraid of a mouse before.

She nodded sharply, then turned and entered the house.

Robin led the way, and we followed.

"I'll just wait out here," the wolf said.

When I got all the way into the house, I had to agree that waiting outside was a pretty good idea. This place was gross. Every surface seemed to be covered in dark grime. Several cauldrons sat on the floor, smoking with dark magic that gleamed green and purple. The hearth flickered with yellow flame, and a large lizard warmed its belly in front of the fire. A long green tongue flicked out as it glared at me with beady eyes.

This was nothing like Lachlan's organized potion workshop. This was pure dark magic.

"What do you want?" Torlock hissed.

I turned to her, taken aback by how she seemed to melt into the wall behind her, becoming one with the creepy workshop.

"We found a Sylthian potion at the site of a crime," Lachlan said. "We know that you're one of the few people who can make them, and we want to know who you sell to."

She grimaced, clearly not wanting to divulge her information.

Robin stepped forward, glaring. "You owe me, Torlock. Answer the questions, and our debt is settled."

She hissed. A few seconds passed.

Come on, creepy lady.

"Fine," she spat. "Only one customer wanted Sylthian potion. About two weeks ago, a demon from Magic's Bend came here, asking about it. Said he needed it for a big job. Just in case he ran into trouble."

The whole of the Protectorate counted as trouble, so it made sense he'd be worried about running into some of us while robbing the castle.

"Magic's Bend?" Lachlan asked, his eyes gleaming with interest. "You're sure?"

"Of course I'm sure. I'm no idiot."

"Never said you were." Robin's voice was soothing. "What else do you know?"

She frowned.

Hmmm. Clearly she knew something else, but didn't want to share. She was a shit actress.

"What can you tell us about him?" Lachlan asked. "His name? What did he look like?"

"Fine. He was a more human-looking demon, with pale skin and sawed-off horns. Blond hair and a slick red coat." She walked to a dirty table. It was so dark and grimy I hadn't even noticed it was there. It pretty much blended in with every other gross thing there.

She pulled a little object off the table and returned to us, holding out the shining gold coin so that we could see. "He paid with this."

I squinted at it, making out the unfamiliar symbol. It looked like some kind of old-fashioned money. "What is it?"

"A coin from Grimaldi's, you moron," Torlock hissed.

"What is Grimaldi's?"

"Gambling den. The demon looked real twitchy, like he was just dying to get back to the tables."

"I've been to Magic's Bend a few times," I said. "I've never seen Grimaldi's. Where is it?"

"Bats if I know." She shrugged. "I've told you everything. Now get out."

"We want the coin," Lachlan said. "We'll pay you double for it."

She frowned, clearly debating. Then she nodded. "Fine. Five hundred dollars."

Lachlan pulled out his wallet and retrieved some bills, then handed them over.

She gave him the coin. "Now be gone with you!"

Robin studied her for a minute more, as if trying to figure out if she was lying. Then he nodded. "All right. Thank you, Torlock. Our debt is settled."

She spit on the ground. In her own house!

Ew.

We made a hasty retreat out of Torlock's creepy lair. I sucked in the clean, fresh air outside.

Fine, it wasn't that clean or that fresh. But compared to inside her house, it was delightful.

The wolf turned from where he was leaning against the wall. "Any luck?"

"Yes. Thanks to Robin, here."

"Excellent." The wolf grinned at the giant mouse. "Well done, pal. Come by for a beer sometime."

"It's a plan." Robin turned to us. "Best of luck with your mission. I must be off now."

"Thank you." I grinned at him, delighted with Robin Hood. A mouse! So much cooler than just a regular old dude.

"Thanks, mate," Lachlan said.

"See you around." Sparkling green magic flared around the mouse again, and he shrank back to his original size, then scampered off down the street.

I turned to Lachlan. "I really like this place."

"Aye, so do I." Lachlan turned to the wolf. "Ready to get out of here?"

"Am I ever," the wolf said. "Just being here makes me feel like I need a bath."

10

———

F ortunately, we didn't have to climb back down the beanstalk. Since we knew where we wanted to go and it wasn't some crazy magical realm, Lachlan was able to make a portal.

We said goodbye to the wolf, who had dressed back up in his grandma dress and bonnet, then departed the fairytale world for earth.

Lachlan made a portal, and I'd never been so grateful to get sucked away. If going up that beanstalk had been hard, I could only imagine that going down was twenty times worse.

The portal delivered me to the lawn in front of Lachlan's house in the French countryside. He'd said that he preferred to live in Scotland, but his best workshop was here.

It was night in France, with the moon high above. A cold breeze drifted over my face, and the air smelled of winter.

Lachlan stepped out of the portal and stopped next to me. "Give me a few moments to check on the tracking potion and the scrap of the cloak. And I'll make a few restorative drafts for Arach, Florian, and the pugs. The drafts won't save them, but they might help them hold on longer."

I turned to him. "Thank you. For everything."

His dark eyes met mine, and a connection sparked between us. It felt like a live wire, pulling us closer together. His gaze lingered longer than necessary, warming me from within.

He blinked, then stepped back.

Clearly, he was fighting some kind of internal battle, because the idea that we couldn't pursue this because we worked together was crap. But I had no idea what the battle was, and I definitely had no idea how to ask.

I swallowed hard and stepped back as well. "Mind if I get a shower?"

"Of course. You know where it is."

I gave him one last look, trying to figure out what it was that I saw in his dark eyes, then turned and went toward the house. Unable to help myself, I snuck one peek at him as he walked toward the large barn that held his potion workshop.

The door to the house opened as I entered, and Mildred the pretty ghost smiled at me.

"You're back!" she said.

"I am indeed."

She gestured me inside. "You're the only woman to ever come here, you know. Besides me and the housekeeper. And now you've come twice!"

"Um, yes." I had no idea what to say to that.

"Well, it's exciting is all. He must really like you."

I had no idea how to answer that. Fortunately, Mildred didn't seem to need a response. She could carry on a conversation just fine without me.

"You know, I really think he seems a bit happier," she said. "It's nothing obvious like smiling. Lord no! But something in his demeanor, you know?"

"What do you mean?" I shut the door behind me, enjoying the warmth of the old farmhouse.

"He just seems more cheerful. He's been here the last couple of days—besides today, of course—working in his workshop on that piece of cloth. Apparently, it's a terribly hard thing to figure out. But anyway, he just seems better somehow."

"That's good."

"Of course it is, you ninny. I think it's because of you!"

"I think you're reaching," I said. "Lachlan and I are just friends. Work colleagues."

"Oh, likely story." She wrinkled her nose as her gaze traveled up and down my form. "You stink of old fish and look like you climbed up a chimney."

I looked down. The smell I'd become used to. But I hadn't realized that Fairy Tale City had also left a coating of sooty magic on me. It was very faint, but Mildred had an eagle eye.

"You'd better get cleaned up." She drifted toward the bedroom. "Come on. Let's get you into a nice dress."

Because Mildred was nice and I was a wimp—and also because I didn't want to smell like old fish—I ended up wearing some of her clothes. The old-timey style wasn't growing on me, but I did like wearing something clean, that was for sure. Not even Muffin would be down with the fish stink that I'd been wearing.

By the time I made it out into the living room, Lachlan stood there, his back to me. His hair was wet and his clothes were clean, so he must have taken the fastest shower in the history of the world.

"Well?" I asked. "How's the tracking potion coming."

He turned, his gaze bright. "The cloaked figure is connected to the theft."

I stopped. "What?"

"The tracking potion finished, and it points to Magic's Bend. It can't be a coincidence."

"Holy crap." I blinked. "That's... Shit, that's not good, is it?"

"Not particularly, no. He—or she—is powerful. They've managed to get into the castle, or send other people in. It's not good news for us."

"No kidding. But maybe we can use this. Now we're hunting two birds in the same bush. Better than two bushes."

He nodded. "We just need to find them."

"And tell the Protectorate. This is a good clue. A *really* good clue."

"Let's go."

I joined him, and he raised his hand to create a portal. This time, however, it took a lot longer for the glowing magic to appear. I glanced up at him, worried, and noted that his face was pale, his eyes drawn.

"What's wrong?" I asked.

"Nothing." He nodded toward the portal, which was finally big enough. "Get in."

I stepped through, letting the ether suck me in and pull me through space, spitting me out on the lawn. Lachlan followed, and was definitely paler when he arrived.

"Seriously, what's wrong?" I demanded.

"I'm fine."

"I'm fine," I mimicked. "Such a man."

"I am a man."

"A man who is not fine. What's wrong? You look like you're low on magic, but we didn't use that much back in the fairytale world."

"I used it to create the restorative drafts."

"Oh." *I got it.* "You put your magic, and your life force, into the potion. Kind of like with the Oblivisi potion."

"Aye. I'll be fine after I sleep."

I smiled. "Well, thank you. Arach and the ghosts will appreciate it." *I* appreciated it. They were my friends, not Lachlan's. But still, he helped them.

"Did you find something?" Jude's voice echoed across the lawn, and I jumped away from Lachlan.

"Yes!" I hurried toward her, noting the stern glint in her eyes. "We found something."

"Good. Because things are getting dire here."

I followed her into the main entry hall, stopping abruptly when I spotted Florian. He floated near the stairs, a forced cheerful expression on his face. But his body was so much more faded. It was like he was half gone already.

Farther up the stairs stood Potts, the day librarian who hated Florian.

Except.... He looked clearly distressed. As if he'd been walking down the stairs, just spotted Florian, and stopped in shock.

Apparently, he didn't hate the night librarian at all.

Oh fates, this was bad, if even Potts was distressed.

"We can't find Chaos," Jude murmured.

"What?" Shocked, I turned to her. "What do you mean?"

"He may be gone. Or hiding. The other pugs are as bad off as Florian, so Chaos must be in bad shape as well. I don't know how much longer they have left."

My heart tore in two for the little horned pug. And for the rest. This was awful. I turned to Lachlan, but he was already striding toward Florian. He held out the little vial that glowed with a ghostly blue light. I'd never heard of a living person managing to make something for a ghost, but Lachlan's talents were unheard of.

"Drink this. It will help a bit," Lachlan said.

Florian nodded and uncorked the bottle, then gulped down the liquid. He glowed briefly, starting to look a little more *there*.

"It won't last very long, but it will buy you some time," Lachlan said. "We'll find Arach's magic. I promise."

"How is she?" I asked Jude.

"In her office, resting. So you have a clue?"

"We do. Whoever—"

Jude held up a hand. "Let's get everyone together so you only have to say it once."

"Okay."

"You look hungry. We'll do it in the kitchen."

My stomach grumbled. "Thanks."

Lachlan and I followed Jude down into Hans's domain. His eyes brightened when he saw us. Boris sat on his shoulder. He waved his little pink paw.

"Sit! I will feed you!" Hans bustled around the kitchen, grabbing things out of cupboards.

We sat, and within moments, there were bowls of hearty soup and cups of juice in front of us. Caro, Ali, and Haris clattered down the stairs into the kitchen, followed by Rowan and Bree, who must've been back from her mission in Ireland. If Mayhem was in danger, I couldn't blame her for hurrying back.

"I heard you found something?" Caro's silver eyes were bright. "What was it?"

"Yeah, spill," Ali said. "Because we struck out."

Everyone found a seat around the big round table, and I explained our meeting with Torlock and the fact that the cloaked figure was in Magic's Bend.

"Magic's Bend?" Jude frowned. "I suppose that makes sense, since it's the biggest magical city in America. But I've never heard of Grimaldi's."

There was a murmur of agreement from around the table. It seemed that no one had heard of it.

"So we need to go there and look around," Caro said. "Track this jerk down using his coin."

"That was my thought." I eyed Jude, wondering if she'd put the hammer down on me going. "I'd like to go ask the FireSouls. They've lived in Magic's Bend for over ten years. If there's something there, they'd know it."

Jude gave me a shrewd look, the wheels clearly turning in her head. She leaned forward. "You know that I didn't agree with you going rogue."

I swallowed hard and nodded.

"But you were right to follow your instincts. The Protectorate runs well because we follow the rules. I gave you freedom last week to hunt with Lachlan, but the other board members were giving me pushback. On one hand, they're right. The rules keep us safe. But sometimes, going rogue helps. In this instance, you may have saved us all." She raised a finger. "Now don't let it go to your head. There'll be no gallivanting off after this. You have to buckle down and finish your training, because Arach and the board make decisions, too, and they insist on the rule. But I'll go to bat for you this time so that you can go find Grimaldi's. But Bree and Caro must go with you. They're both official members of the PITs, so they'll help keep an eye on things."

I grinned. I didn't mind working with Bree, and Caro was the bomb. "Thank you, Jude."

She nodded. "Thank *you*. But be careful. This won't be easy. And we need you back here in one piece."

After the meeting, Lachlan gave the three restorative drafts to Bree. I prayed that someone found Chaos so that he could take the potion.

Worry tugged at me as we climbed the stairs back to the main entry hall. At the top, Bree and Rowan rushed off to find the pugs. Most people in the castle were hunting for Chaos, and

I crossed my fingers that they would find him. Jude had ordered me to sleep, and I couldn't say that I hated the idea. I was about to fall over, and I needed to be fresh for the next morning when we went looking for Grimaldi's.

Of course, Rowan was going to come. She hadn't bothered asking permission, but she hadn't officially started at the Academy yet, so she could do what she wanted.

In the main entry hall, I stopped, grabbing Lachlan's arm. "Hey, stop."

He turned to me.

"Where are you sleeping?" I asked.

"I'll find a place. Maybe in the city." He seemed to sway slightly on his feet. "I'll take the portal in the forest."

As I'd guessed, he'd completely drained himself making the potions for the ghosts. He didn't have the magic left to make a portal, so he'd take one of the ready-made ones into Edinburgh. Except that would cut off at least an hour or two of his sleep time.

"You can stay with me," I said.

His eyes widened just slightly.

"On my couch." *Idiot.* I should have made that clear. The last thing I needed was Lachlan thinking I was coming on to him. "I have a great couch. And we're colleagues, so it's fine."

Yeah, that was a stellar example of saying too much to try to diffuse the awkwardness and only make it worse.

"Ah." He hesitated briefly, but I could tell that he wanted to stay. It was clear as day on his face. "Aye, I will. Thanks."

"Great." I turned and started walking toward my apartment, assuming that he'd come along.

Yeah, we were just colleagues. *Totally.*

Except that the truth was staring us right in the face, and we were both just ignoring it.

We weren't just colleagues. We might not be acting on

anything, but we weren't just colleagues. I blushed to the roots of my hair, so hot I could feel it.

Get it together, nerd.

The hall was quiet as we walked, which just made the tension in the air thicker. I pushed open the door to my tower and led the way up to my apartment. It was empty inside, with no cats on the couch. Normally, they'd be there, and I'd been wondering what kind of complex bargaining I'd have to perform to get them to vacate for Lachlan.

It was unnecessary, apparently. Maybe they were running a racket down at the docks, or robbing a jewelry store on the Royal Mile.

I swept out a hand. "Well, this is it."

"It's lovely," Lachlan said.

And he was right. It was. I still marveled at the pretty apartment the castle had created for me.

Lachlan's gaze traveled across the artwork on the walls. "You did those?"

"Most."

"You're very talented."

"Thanks."

His eyes fell on the painting of the dead mouse that Princess Snowflake III had made for me. "That one is...interesting."

I grinned. "A present. From Princess."

"Ah."

I pointed to the couch, which already had a blanket draped over the back. "Well, that's yours. Help yourself to anything in the kitchen. Don't let the cats bully you."

"I'll do my best."

I turned to go, but he reached for my arm, gripping gently.

I turned, looking up at him. My breath caught in my throat.

"Thank you." His voice was soft.

"Yeah. No problem." I tried to keep my eyes off his lips. It wasn't easy.

His own gaze flickered down just briefly, then he let go of me.

My heart thundered as I hurried up the stairs. As soon as I reached the top, I closed my eyes and tried to get myself under control. I was being ridiculous. Acting like a teenager.

Lachlan was just a dude.

Well, not a *dude* really. A man. Definitely a man.

A man that I was losing my mind over.

Sighing at my own ridiculousness, I opened my eyes.

The Cats of Catastrophe stared at me. All three were sitting on my bed, leaving almost no room left for me.

Well, that was no surprise.

11

T he dream came quickly and quietly, so subtle that I didn't realize it was a dream at all. One moment I was in my bed, the next, I was walking barefoot across the cold wet grass outside of the castle.

The stone circle was calling me, and I was powerless to resist.

Wind whipped at my hair, blowing off the sea so strongly that it threatened to carry me away. But I kept going, drawn by the circle that was bathed in the moonlight. The stones repelled me normally, but today, they called.

The stones rose tall, piercing the night sky and looming overhead.

They seemed bigger, as tall as skyscrapers.

Or maybe they were just bigger to me, because they were so important. This place had called to me before, but I'd resisted, repelled by something.

But I could resist no longer.

I kept going, the wind cold against my skin.

Magic sparked on the air as I neared, something unfamiliar,

yet not. At one moment, I could have sworn I'd never felt it before. Then another, it was totally familiar.

My steps slowed as I neared the circle, nerves making my hair stand on end.

Determined, I stepped closer, stopping at the edge. I laid a hand on the massive rock, feeling magic spark up my arm.

Though I was tempted to step inside, I didn't dare. There was too much magic in there. Too much risk.

The center of the circle glowed golden and bright. I shielded my eyes, squinting.

A figure appeared within, the same one that had appeared to me in the fairytale world.

"You," I said.

"Aye, Ana Blackwood. I have called you here, through your dreams."

"Why? What do you want from me?"

"What every god wants of a Dragon God."

"So you *are* a god. Which one?"

"Sulis."

"I don't recognize that."

"That is not a surprise. We are an ancient religion, with many factions and many gods."

"But which—"

A shriek sounded, and a light flashed, cutting off my question. At the edge the circle, a figure hurtled toward Sulis. Another ghost.

The golden figure of the god disappeared, leaving nothing but the one who had tried to attack.

I blinked, shocked. "Mom?"

The ghost turned to me, so familiar it made me ache. I reached out to her.

"Ana, you must go! Never come to the circle."

"But what do you—"

Thunder cracked and lightning struck, shooting from the sky as a bright white bolt.

It struck my mother's ghost, lighting her up like a bonfire. She collapsed.

Something inside me tore. I screamed, starting forward, but she reached out a hand.

"No!" The command in her voice stopped me. "Too dangerous." Her voice was weak, ragged. "I would save you from this."

Tears poured down my face, a ragged sob bursting forth. "But I need my Dragon God power. I need to know what I am. I need to help you!"

I had to go to her. I stepped forward.

"No! Don't chase it, Ana. Too deadly. Too much." The plea in her voice stopped me.

"Deadly to others? To you?" I couldn't hurt my mother.

"To you."

Thunder cracked again. This time, the lightning exploded in a burst of light. It struck from the sky, landing directly on her. She screamed. I screamed.

She disappeared.

I gasped, my own shriek waking me. I bolted out of bed, sweating and shaky.

My eyes popped open, meeting Lachlan's immediately.

I screamed again, but I had no breath and it came out as a wispy thing.

Lachlan gripped my shoulders, his touch grounding me in reality. "Ana! Ana, are you all right?"

Gasping, I blinked, trying to get it together.

That had been a *dream.*

But I'd seen my mother. She'd really been there.

Tears sprang to my eyes.

She'd been struck by lightning. Twice.

Tears rolled down my face, and I gasped. Losing her once had been hard enough. We'd been only thirteen, still on the run from those who had hunted us. Mom had taken us away.

Then they'd found us.

She'd bought us time, letting us escape.

But she hadn't made it.

And I'd just watched her die again. The sobs tore through me, ragged and harsh.

Lachlan pulled me close, hugging me. I gripped him, unable to let go, and sobbed. The Cats of Catastrophe, who'd clearly vacated the bed when I'd had my freak-out, leapt on and pressed themselves against me. Even Princess.

Lachlan petted my hair. His touch sent waves of calm through me, slowing my sobs and my shaking.

"A nightmare?" he asked.

"It didn't start as one." Reluctantly, I pulled back. I needed to get it together. I scrubbed the tears from my face. "It almost seemed like I was going to learn what I was."

Lachlan didn't say anything, though he had to be curious. I'd alluded to getting new magic, but I'd never said exactly what I was. He might have guessed. Maybe.

But either way, I no longer felt weird about telling him. He'd had my back during the last week, never failing. He'd given his magic to the ghosts, and never faltered when the Cheshire cat had tried to give him his heart's desire in exchange for me.

"I'm a Dragon God," I said.

His eyes widened briefly. "That's something."

I chuckled weakly. "Isn't it? But I have no idea what pantheon I'm part of. I think I was about to find out in the dream. I think one of the gods called me there. He was called Sulis." I really needed to get into the library to figure out who the heck he was. "But then my mother appeared, driving him away."

"She did?"

I nodded. "Her ghost, at least. Or her spirit. I don't know. I told you that she was killed when I was thirteen." I sucked in a ragged breath, blinking to keep the tears in my eyes. The last thing I needed was more weeping. "But I didn't mention that she was murdered."

Grief flashed in his eyes. Not pity, but grief. The empath in him?

"I was being hunted by someone who wanted me because I was a Dragon God." My sisters, too, though I didn't mention them. I trusted him not to reveal them, but protecting them was second nature, and it was easier just not to bring them up. "My mother sacrificed herself to let us get away. Then she came back now, sacrificing herself again to keep the god from telling me which pantheon I'm part of. She doesn't want me to know."

"Why not?"

"She was a powerful seer, so she must have seen something."

"She fears it's too dangerous."

"How'd you know?"

"It's not hard to guess. She died to protect you the first time, so she'd do it again. Danger to you could bring her to this plane."

I nodded, my mind playing the lightning strike over and over again, like a horrible movie. Tears spilled over my eyelids. I clenched my teeth and scrubbed them away, pissed at myself.

"I'm such a wimp," I muttered.

"I'd say you're human." He smiled. "And you're tough. Stalwart. You never complain. You always take care of business. Those are all very *unwimpy* qualities."

A smile tugged at my lips. "You sound like you don't use the word wimp very often."

"I can't say that I do." He gave me one last look, searching my eyes to make sure that I was all right.

I tried to give him a reassuring smile, which he seemed to buy, thank fates.

He stood. "Ready to find Grimaldi's?"

"Totally."

We met everyone in the main entryway at eight a.m., as planned. Bree, Rowan, and Caro waited for us, each holding a steaming cup of coffee. Bree and Rowan each held an extra cup, and I eyed them hopefully.

I grinned when Bree passed one off to me. Rowan handed one to Lachlan, raising her brows.

The question was clear. *Why the heck are you coming downstairs with my sister early in the morning?*

He just smiled and murmured, "Thanks."

I chugged the coffee, nearly burning my throat, then said, "Everyone ready?"

There was a chorus of yeses, and we all set our coffee cups on a ledge. Eventually, they'd magically disappear back to the kitchen, a spell that I wished my apartment had.

As a group, we set off toward the enchanted forest. There was a portal there that would take us straight to Magic's Bend.

Lachlan led the way through the twisted old trees. Though the sun was bright in the sky, it was shadowed and cool in here, the fairy lights dancing in the air. It smelled of damp earth and greenery, a scent that I was growing to love.

Rowan grabbed my arm to slow my walk, and I looked at her, confused. Caro hurried ahead, starting to talk to Lachlan, while Bree hung back with me and Rowan.

Ah, of course. "Question time?"

"Duh," Rowan said.

I eyed Caro's back. Clearly, my sisters had put her up to distracting Lachlan.

"So..." Bree whispered. "He came down from your room this morning."

"Nothing happened."

"You don't let strangers sleep in your apartment," Rowan said.

"We're not strangers. We're colleagues."

"Like Cade and I were colleagues?" Bree said.

"That's different." I scowled. She and Cade had ended up together. It was clear to anyone that they were a perfect match. Me and Lachlan?

Yeah, I might've wanted to jump on him, but that didn't mean we were the perfect match.

"It doesn't seem different," Bree said.

"Well, it is."

"I've seen the way he looks at you," Rowan said. "It's not platonic. Let me tell you that."

"Well, we've made a no-kissing rule."

"So that means you kissed?" Rowan asked.

"It means they kissed." Bree nodded knowingly.

I sighed. "It was a quick one." But the best of my life, hands down. "Then he said we couldn't do it again because we work together."

"Ah, I'm familiar with that one," Bree said. "It won't stick."

"Yes, it will. I'm a professional. I want to become a full member of the Protectorate. I'm not going to screw this up."

"It's not *technically* against the rules," Bree said. "And he doesn't even work for the Protectorate."

"I know that." I scowled. "But I can't worry about any of that right now."

"True story," Rowan said. "You've got bigger shit to worry about. Like this cloaked figure and Arach's heart.

We'd just reached the clearing in the woods where the three portals hovered in midair. Two were active—the glowing blue one went to Edinburgh, and the white one to Magic's Bend. A third was dark and dormant. It had once led to a fae realm, but had since been blocked off from permanent access. One could still get through, but it was difficult.

We lined up in front of the white portal and stepped through one at a time. I went last, and the ether sucked me up and spun me around, carrying me through space and spitting me out in a dark alley.

My friends were already at the edge of the alley, and I hurried to join them, not enjoying the distinct scent of pee that permeated the place. The portal put us out in the Historic District, which was the oldest part of Magic's Bend. It was also the party district, where restaurants and bars crowded into the old buildings.

As a result, the alleys acted as last-minute bathrooms for the supernaturals stumbling home from the bars late at night.

It was gross.

When I reached the street, I sucked in a breath of fresher air. There were still a lot of supernaturals out. With the time change, it was still party hour here. Magic's Bend had a totally different feel that even the supernatural district of Edinburgh lacked. There, we had a neighborhood within a bigger human city. Humans couldn't find it, of course. But people were still aware that there were non-magical folk nearby.

Not in Magic's Bend, though. There were no humans for a hundred miles. The little city was blocked by a charm, and as a result, the supernaturals were one hundred percent comfortable with walking around with their wings or their horns on display. I definitely liked it.

"Lachlan's getting a cab," Bree said.

"Good." We'd have to go a few miles to Factory Row, where the FireSouls had their shop, and I didn't want to hoof it.

When a glittering purple car pulled up to the curb, we all piled in. The pink leather seat in the back extended magically to accommodate the four of us girls, while Lachlan took the front. A pixie with green hair grinned into the rearview mirror.

"Where are we off to?" she asked.

"Ancient Magic, on Factory Row," Lachlan said.

"All righty." She hit the gas, and the cab jumped away from the curb. "I seem to deliver a lot of people to that shop."

"Popular place," Lachlan said.

"Don't I know it," she said. "Those three who work there run a good business."

That was the truth.

"What do they sell?" Caro asked.

"They're treasure hunters," I said. "They find enchanted artifacts and sell the magic inside."

"That's illegal," Caro said. "You can't just wander up to an archaeological site and take stuff."

"Right. They only take the artifacts with the most decayed magic." Over time, magic degraded. "They take the ones that are about to explode, then remove the magic and put it in a replica artifact. That's what they sell. Then they return the original artifact to the archaeological site. They've got a permit for it and everything."

"I like it," Caro said. "That's really freaking clever."

"And hopefully they'll be able to tell us where Grimaldi's is." I leaned toward the cab driver. "Do you know where Grimaldi's is?"

She glanced into the rearview mirror. "Never heard of it."

I leaned back. It was weird that a cab driver wouldn't know, but I wasn't that surprised. Things were never so easy.

A few minutes later, we arrived on Factory Row, a street on the outskirts of town that had once been the industrial center of Magic's Bend in the nineteenth century. Sometime recently, the old warehouses and factories had been converted into trendy apartments and shops.

We passed by Potions & Pastilles, where Connor and Claire worked, and the cab pulled over in front of Ancient Magic.

We piled out of the car and approached the wide glass window of the shop. Hopefully someone would be there, because otherwise I'd be throwing rocks at their windows. Cass, Nix, and Del all lived above Ancient Magic, each inhabiting one of the upper three floors of the building. Cass usually handled most of the treasure hunting, with the occasional help from Del, while Nix ran the front counter.

I strode up to the window, peering between the scrolled golden letters that spelled out *Ancient Magic*.

Behind the desk, a dark-haired woman was fiddling with something small. Nix.

I reached for the door handle and pulled, but it was locked.

Nix looked up, catching my gaze through the glass door. She grinned and hurried forward, then unlocked the door and pulled it open. A cartoon cat grinned out at me from her T-shirt. Despite the fact that she was seriously badass, you wouldn't necessarily know it. She always wore cat T-shirts, and never looked as strong as she actually was.

"Hey!" Nix said. "We aren't open this late, sorry. But come in!"

"Thanks." I smiled and entered the little shop, my friends following behind me as I headed toward the desk, careful not to bump into any of the artifacts that were stacked on the floor or set onto little tables.

Nix went behind the counter, her gaze traveling over all of us. "I can't imagine this is a late night shopping trip."

"Not exactly," I said.

"Though I do like your shop." Caro wandered around, peeking at the different objects that Nix had conjured to match the original artifacts. With her skillset, she was the perfect one to man the desk here. Cass would bring her the artifacts, and Nix would conjure a replica and move the magic over.

"Thanks." Nix propped her hands on the counter. "What can I do for you?"

"Do you know where Grimaldi's is?" Lachlan asked.

Nix frowned. "Never heard of it. Is it supposed to be here?"

"Somewhere in Magic's Bend," he said. "It's a casino."

"We don't have any casinos."

I tugged the golden coin out of my pocket and pushed it across the desk toward her. "Is this familiar?"

Her eyes lit up at the sight of the gold—the dragon in her, no doubt—but she frowned almost immediately.

"I don't recognize it." She picked it up and turned it over, her frown deepening. "And my dragon sense isn't picking anything up either."

Ah, crap. That was Plan B.

I described the coin's original owner, hoping that the info would help ignite her dragon sense, but she just shook her head.

Dang.

I'd gotten the impression that Grimaldi's might be kind of secret. But we had the coin. FireSouls could track almost anything, but only if it wasn't protected by a concealment charm of some kind.

"So it's got a concealment charm on it?" Rowan asked.

"It does. A strong one." She closed her eyes, her magic swelling on the air.

I waited, my breath held. Everyone else seemed tense as well.

Nix's eyes popped open. "Yeah, my third try was *not* the charm. I'm still getting nothing."

Dang it.

The door behind us creaked open, and a lilting voice echoed into the shop. "Hello, ladies. Was I not invited to the party?"

I turned, catching sight of Aerdeca waltzing into the shop. Her usual white pantsuit was impeccably crisp, and her blond hair fell over her shoulder like a sleek waterfall. Her magic rolled out from her in a wave, deceptively sweet with its sound of chirping birds and the feel of a spring breeze.

The Blood Sorceress smiled at us, and it was a bit shark-like.

"Aerdeca," Nix said. "What brings you here so late?"

"I need a birthday present for Mordaca, so I had to sneak out while she was on a date." Her gaze sharpened on the coin in Nix's hand. The color drained from her face. "Where'd you get that?"

Nix pointed to us. "They're looking for a place called Grimaldi's."

Aerdeca turned to us, her face stark. I'd never seen her scared before. She was a stone-cold, badass bitch, and I meant that as the highest compliment. I'd seen her face down demons without flinching, coming away with her white suit coated in their blood. But *this* little thing scared her?

"Why the hell would you want to go there?" she asked. "It's a hellhole."

"So it's really in Magic's Bend?" Nix asked. "I've never heard of it."

"You wouldn't," she said. "It's not your kind of place."

"But it's yours?" Nix asked.

It was clear what she was saying. Aerdeca and Mordaca lived and worked in Darklane, where the dark magic practitioners lived. If you were going to be bad, that's where you hung out. But

Aerdeca and Mordaca weren't that bad, despite the fact that they were scary as hell.

"It was," Aerdeca said. "But we escaped that life."

"Escaped?" That was a heavy freaking word.

"Escaped." Aerdeca nodded. "And never went back. I'd advise you to do the same."

"We can't. Something valuable has been stolen, and we need to get it back. Our only lead is at Grimaldi's."

"There's nothing valuable enough to go there," Aerdeca said.

"There is." I told her about Arach and the ghosts and the Protectorate's magic.

Aerdeca frowned, indecision flashing across her face. She hesitated. "Fine. That is compelling. And it makes sense that Arach's heart would go to Grimrealm."

"Grimrealm?" Lachlan asked.

"That's where the casino is located. Grimrealm is an underground black market and neighborhood. And I mean *black*. You think Darklane is bad? It's nothing. Sure, dark magic happens there. Bad people and crime and shit you don't want to mess with. But Grimrealm is where all the *really* bad shit happens."

"And you spent time there?" Nix asked, clearly trying to get to the bottom of the mystery that was Aerdeca and Mordaca.

"We were born there." She shuddered. "Anyway, Grimrealm's market is famous. If you wanted to sell some powerful magic, that is where you'd go. It's completely under the radar, and absolutely awful."

"So they're selling Arach's heart." Bile rose in my throat. She was my friend. And they wanted to *sell* her *heart*.

Bastards.

"It's the best place to do it," Aerdeca said. "But it's going to be hard to get in. You'll stand out like a sore thumb with your magical signature."

Shit. She had a point. "So there are no normal people there?"

"In Grimrealm, being evil *is* normal. You're going to have to figure something out if you want to pass. Otherwise, they'll kick you right out. And that's what they'd do if you're lucky. I'd put money on them killing you instead." She nodded, eyes turned back toward the past. "Yes. I think they'd kill you."

"But you can tell us how to get there?" Bree asked.

"Not exactly, no. When we escaped, we were smuggled out in barrels."

Barrels? Holy fates, talk about desperate measures.

"I didn't see exactly how we got out," Aerdeca sad. "And we were just teenagers, anyway. But I do know that the entrance is through Fairlight Alley, next to Darklane. That's where they took us out of the barrels. Mordaca was having a panic attack, so we didn't make it all the way to the safe house."

They'd needed a safe house? What the hell was in Aerdeca and Mordaca's past?

"So, somehow, we can get from that alley into Grimrealm," I said, studiously avoiding the topic of Aerdeca's past. I wanted to tell her I was sorry for the shit she'd been through as a teenager —hell, I knew *all* about that—but it was obvious she wouldn't welcome it.

"Yes. Somehow." She shrugged. "But I can't help you with that. The only thing I can really tell you is that you're going to need a damned good disguise. Something that will hide your magical signatures and make it look like you're evil enough to be down there. They won't trust anyone who doesn't stink like dark magic."

"I can help with that." Nix reached under the counter and pulled out a snake-shaped dagger. The magic that wafted off of it smelled like the bottom of a sewer. Even the Paris sewer hadn't smelled this bad. Worse, it was overlaid with the scent of sulfur. "Cass just brought this back from a temple in Indonesia. A powerful dark wizard imbued it with some kinda gross murder charm. We can't sell it, obviously, but the magic in the dagger is almost completely decayed, so we couldn't leave it in the temple like that. It would have blown the place up eventually."

"Do we carry it with us?" I asked.

"No. We want to put the original dagger back in the temple. I'll put the magic into a set of cloaks. It'll shroud your own signature. And if it's broken up, it won't be so dangerous, so the spell probably won't explode."

"And take us with it."

She grinned. "Exactly. When you're done, burn the cloaks."

"Perfect." This was going to be dangerous, but excitement welled in my chest. We had a solid plan.

12

A couple of hours later, after Aerdeca had given us as much information as she could about Grimrealm and Nix had created the disgusting, dark magic-soaked cloaks for us, we headed over to Darklane.

Aerdeca gave us a ride in her white Cadillac, dropping us off near the entrance of Fairlight Alley. There was a late night carnival, and the crowded streets were bustling with people. We were right at the edge of Darklane here, so the stalls selling goods were a mix of normal citizens and Darklaners.

Aerdeca leaned out the driver's side window. "Good luck."

"Thanks again. I hope Mordaca likes her present."

Aerdeca tried to smile, but worry still flickered in her eyes. Worry for us. What had happened to her down in Grimrealm?

I doubted she'd ever tell me.

She pulled away from the curb, and I turned to my friends. We each had a cloak clutched in our hands—no way we were putting them on until absolutely necessary. All around us, the streets were heaving with people.

"Ready?" I asked.

"Born ready." Bree grinned cheerily.

I chuckled.

We pushed our way through the crowd, heading toward the entrance to Fairlight Alley. As we neared, the crowd thinned. My stomach turned slightly, and I felt a strong compulsion to back away from the alley.

"Repelling charm," Lachlan said.

I gritted my teeth and headed forward. There were no people standing in front of the alley, as if they'd all agreed that this section of the sidewalk sucked, and they'd stay ten feet away.

Bree grabbed my hand. "I'm going to keep guard here, where the people are standing. It'll look too weird if I stand right outside the alley. No one in their right mind would stand in the middle of that charm."

I nodded. "Good plan."

Since we didn't know what we were walking into, we'd decided that Bree would stand out here and keep watch for a few minutes.

She stayed behind, squished between a man wearing a balloon animal hat and a woman in old witch's robes. The rest of us put on our cloaks. The stench immediately made my eyes water, but the feel of it was worse. The cloak, which was a dark green wool, felt like it was made of spiders crawling over my skin.

"Ugh, this is the worst," Rowan said.

"Worse than jumping into a pit full of worms." Caro flipped the cloak up over her platinum hair.

I did the same, immediately wanting to tear the thing off and jump in the ocean. Lachlan was stoically silent, of course, but I caught the shudder that ran through him.

"Let's get this over with," I muttered.

We headed toward the alley, striding over like we knew what we were doing. Unlike the alleys in the Historic District, this one didn't smell like pee. It didn't smell like much of anything, actually, which was pretty weird.

And it wasn't very deep. We got about forty feet back, and it dead-ended into a brick wall.

"Well, that sucks," Caro said.

I stared hard at the wall, remembering Paris. I reached out, pressing my hand against the brick. It was rough against my hand, so it was definitely real.

Maybe.

I pressed hard.

My hand sank into the brick.

"Nice," Rowan said.

I stepped through the wall, having to really work for it. My heart thundered in my ears as I appeared on the other side, ready to draw my weapons from the ether.

There was nothing here.

Just an alley, like the one we'd left behind.

My friends appeared next to me, having fought their way through the illusion of the brick wall.

"Not what I expected," Rowan said.

I approached the end of the alley, which was another forty or so feet in the distance. This time, it was obviously the true dead end. No matter how hard I pressed on the wall, I couldn't get through.

"There's got to be a clue somewhere," Caro said.

We began to search the walls, and the ground, but it was all just brick and stone. Not even an old cigarette butt.

"Hey, look at that." Rowan shined her lightstone ring at the ground, holding it at an angle. She pointed to the indention of a square.

"That's got to be a door of some kind," Caro said.

"Which means there might be some kind of mechanism to

open it." I inspected the walls, searching for anything out of the ordinary.

"Or a password," Lachlan said. "Though perhaps that's not the wisest way to permit access to an underground market. What if they need to change it?"

"Fingers crossed that it's not a password," Caro said.

I stood right over the trapdoor, spinning in a circle as I inspected the walls around me, using my lightstone ring to illuminate the brick. I unfocused my gaze slightly, hoping to catch a pattern if I wasn't looking too hard in one direction.

At first, it just made me vaguely queasy. Then I caught sight of a few bricks in the opposing walls that looked smoother than the others. I approached one, resting my fingertips against it. Yep. Smoother.

"Guys, I think I found something," I said.

Caro appeared at my side a second later. "Twenty bucks you have to press these bricks in a certain order to open the trapdoor."

"But there are three on this wall and three on the other wall," Rowan said. "There are 720 permutations."

"What?" Caro asked.

"There are 720 different orders in which we could press the bricks," Rowan said. She'd always liked math, saying that it was a certain thing in an uncertain world.

"I'd bet good money that you only get one shot," Lachlan said.

"Then how do we figure out the order?" Caro asked.

I inspected each of the bricks. They were all worn down evenly, so that gave no clues.

"If we had a spell that could reveal the past, we could turn back time and watch someone else enter," Rowan said. "But those spells are hard to come by."

"Can you make one?" I asked Lachlan.

"If I had two days. The magic takes a long time to brew."

"We don't have two days." Arach, Florian, and the Pugs of Destruction didn't have a two days.

"Incoming." Bree's voice crackled out of my comms charm. "Two demons."

"Shit, Bree. Can you make us invisible?" I asked, unsure whether her power could extend all the way back here.

"I can try."

"Get by the walls, everyone." I pressed myself against the back wall, far enough away from the trapdoor and the special bricks. My friends joined me, and we stood frozen, shoulder to shoulder.

When our breathing went dead silent, I realized that Lachlan had used his ability to repress sound. A second later, my friends disappeared. So did I. I couldn't even see my legs.

Jackpot.

We stood stiff as boards, tension thick in the air.

A moment later, two demons sauntered into the alley. They looked comfortable as could be, as if they came here regularly. The biggest one, some kind of blue demon that probably had control over ice, if his chill, foggy breath were any indication, went straight for one of the special bricks.

My heart raced as he pressed each brick in order, walking from one side of the wall and back again. The trapdoor in the middle of the floor opened up, and he and his friend jumped right in.

I debated following, but the thing closed almost immediately.

"Jackpot!" Rowan grinned.

I touched the charm at my neck. "Bree? You can come back here now. We know how to get in."

"On my way."

"Okay, everyone. Line up around the trapdoor," I said. "We'll all jump in at the same time. That thing closes real quick."

My friends lined up around the door, Bree joining them when she arrived. I went to the wall and hovered my hand over the first brick.

"Ready?" I asked.

They adjusted their cloaks, and there was a chorus of yeses. I pressed my fingertips to the first brick, then moved quickly to the next. Within ten seconds, I'd pressed them all. Magic sparked around the trapdoor, and it opened.

I hurried over, and we all jumped in.

My heart thundered as I fell, but I landed easily a few seconds later, some kind of magic slowing my descent.

I shuddered at the feeling of dark magic filling the space. It was like my cloak, but it was *everywhere*.

The tunnel that we'd entered was hewn straight out of the dark earth. Torches flickered from the sconces on the wall, green magic providing enough light to see by. The demons were long gone, fortunately, and the tunnel extended into the darkness.

I breathed shallowly against the stench of dark magic, shivering again at the feeling of it crawling over my skin.

"They must have a powerful spell to keep this feeling from spilling out into Magic's Bend," Bree said.

"No kidding," Rowan said. "This would have the Order of the Magica investigating in a hurry."

Lachlan looked at me. "Ready?"

"Yeah, let's get a move on."

As a group, we headed down the tunnel, our footsteps silent. Tension prickled across my skin. Any minute, we could run into other patrons of the Grimrealm. Would our disguises work? Down here, it'd be damned hard to escape if they all turned on us.

We'd walked for only a couple minutes when more magic prickled against my skin.

Like a warning.

Rowan gasped. "Something's coming."

A blast of flame shot from the wall, right in front of us.

I threw out my shield, the white magic bursting forth. For once, my magic obeyed me. The fire slammed into the shield, making my arms shake. It was fierce and orange, filling the whole cavern in front of us.

"Holy fates, good work, Ana." Caro's face was stark.

"You saved us from becoming barbecue," Rowan said.

I chuckled weakly, studying the flame. It wouldn't let up, just kept blazing against my shield.

Next to me, Lachlan crouched down. He was running his hand over a small mound of earth right next to the wall. "I think we were supposed to step on this to keep the flame from blasting us." He pressed on the mound of earth, but the flame didn't stop. "I think this stopped the flame from coming. But now that it's started..."

"It won't stop," I said.

"I've got it." Caro held out her hands, her magic swelling on the air. "Everyone back up."

We did as she commanded, though I was careful to keep the shield up.

"Okay, drop it!" Caro said.

I let my magic fade, and the shield disappeared. The flame roared forth, almost encapsulating Caro. Huge jets of water burst from her palms. It doused the flame, filling the tunnel with steam.

I choked, the steam seeming to make the stench of my cloak even worse. When it finally faded, the tunnel looked totally normal. Caro had hit it with the perfect amount of water. There wasn't even a puddle on the floor.

"Nicely done," I said.

Caro brushed her hands together. "Kind of an expert with the H2O."

Lachlan stepped on the mound of dirt, and a spark of magic glittered in the air. "I think that should do it."

I raised my hands and called on my protective shield, forming a bubble around us. "Just in case."

The shield held strong, and I grinned. My little bit of practice with Lachlan had definitely helped. I made sure to focus on *why* I wanted this magic—to keep us from becoming crispy critters—and the shield held strong.

We entered the section of tunnel that had been flaming. There wasn't a single sound of breathing, so everyone was clearly as nervous as I was, even with the shield.

About a hundred yards later, when I heard the sounds of people, I dropped the shield.

"*That* was intense," Bree said.

"Well, hold on to your butts, because I think it's going to get a lot more intense." Rowan pointed to the glow of magic that lit up the exit to the tunnel. "I think we're here."

I adjusted my cloak, making sure that most of my face was covered. Everyone else followed suit. We approached the edge of the tunnel, walking with a brisk stride. As we neared the exit, I caught sight of masses of people.

If I'd been worried that wearing a full-body cloak would be suspicious, I didn't have to be. More than half the people in the market were wearing cloaks. Apparently, if you dealt in stuff that was this dark, you didn't want to be identified.

The market itself was wild—black tents filled the space, with colorful signs floating above them. They advertised everything from potions to charms to weapons and clothing. People clustered around them, filling the walkways to bursting.

All of it stank like the inside of an old dumpster that had

been eaten by a giant fish that was now rotting, and I sucked air in shallowly.

Didn't dark magic users wonder why they stank so bad?

Seriously, could anything be worse than this stench?

"I can't believe someone is trying to sell Arach's heart down here." Horror echoed in Bree's voice.

"We'll stop them." Lachlan's tone was firm. "Then we'll report this shithole to the Order of the Magica."

My gaze darted around the market. The stalls and people blocked a lot of my view, but the market was obviously huge. On the edges of the open space, there were shops set right into the rock, using the earth for walls.

"It reminds me a bit of Hider's Haven in Death Valley," Bree said.

"Just a lot bigger," Rowan added.

They were right. We'd only been in the haven once—it was actually the topic of the story I'd tried to tell the bullfrog—but the haven had been a much smaller, a less evil version of this place.

I stepped out into the market. "Let's find Grimaldi's. Stick close together. If you get separated, leave."

Together, we pushed our way through the crowd. The feeling here was just plain *dark*. Like I was in a nightmare come to life. I brushed past a few people, and terrible images flashed in my mind. Death and torture.

Were they sending those thoughts into my head? I squeezed my eyes shut and shook my head.

A strong hand gripped my own. Immediately, I knew that it was Lachlan. His comforting touch helped force away some of the images. I clung to it. All around, objects sat on tables. Weapons, grimoires, potions—mostly poisons, from the look of them. And a whole lot of things I didn't recognize, and didn't *want* to recognize.

Dozens of scents hit my nose. We passed a food vendor, and the savory scent actually smelled good. Which somehow made the whole situation worse, once it mixed with the nasty scent of dark magic. I didn't want to find *anything* appealing about this place. Not even hot dogs.

Vendors shouted at customers as we passed, hawking their potions and spells. I ignored them all, until an old woman caught my free hand, pulling me away from Lachlan.

I looked down, startled. She wore a black cloak over her stooped frame, and her black eyes seemed to see right into my soul. "Dearie, dearie, I'll tell your fortune!"

"No thanks."

She gripped me harder, her dark eyes burning. "Dearie, you should listen to your elders. You'll learn things you want to know."

A chill ran over my spine.

Somehow, I believed her.

Maybe it was her magic, but I *really* believed her. I sank onto the little stool in front of her tent.

"What are you doing?" Bree hissed.

"Is this safe?" Lachlan gripped my shoulder. Even his touch couldn't shake me away from the fortune teller's grip.

Her eyes continued to burn into mine.

"Just a moment, guys." I could hear them grumbling, but I only had eyes for the fortune teller as she swept around the little table and sat behind it. She leaned toward me, holding out a wizened hand. For a moment, it looked smooth and young, then it flashed back to old.

"Give me your hand, dearie."

I did as she asked, letting her grip my palm. But she didn't study it, reading the lines and creases that I thought fortune tellers would normally go right for.

Instead, she stared hard into my eyes. My brain seemed to vibrate, and it felt like she was looking right into my soul.

"You'll find what you seek in the circle of stones." Her voice wrapped around me, sending a shiver across my skin.

"What do you mean?"

"Questions you want answered will be revealed to you within the circle."

She meant the stone circle at the Protectorate. She had to. I wanted to ask more—did she know which pantheon I was from? Did she know if my mother was still around in her ghostly form?

No.

Selfish.

I was here for Arach.

"But I'm looking for Grimaldi's," I said.

The fortune teller's eyes flicked to mine. Confusion, then understanding. "Of course." She pointed behind me, and I turned.

There, at the edge of the market, was a sign high in the air. A circle of glittery red stones gleamed in the light.

I turned back to her. "That's it?"

"That's their symbol. Go there and you'll find what you seek."

"So you...you didn't mean that I'd find answers about my past in the circle of stones?"

"Things always have more than one meaning." She stood and held out her hand.

I pressed a wad of cash into it, and she seemed pleased. I turned to my friends, all of whom watched me with concern.

"Let's go," I said.

Together, we pushed through the crowded market, headed toward the casino. My mind raced over what the fortune teller had said, but as we neared the edge of the market, I shoved the thoughts away.

We'd have to be alert for this. Totally on our game. Casinos in the human realm often had tons of security, and I doubted this would be any different. It wouldn't be nearly as easy to blend in the casino.

The stalls thinned out a bit toward the edge, and we lingered briefly near one that sold some kind of strange-smelling beverage that bubbled in an iron cauldron. The casino was one of the buildings that had been built right into the earth, and it was unmarked besides the glittering circle of red stones that were stuck into the rock wall above the door.

Two burly guards stood at the entrance, each wearing a dark green suit. They had their hands crossed in front of them and their cold stares directed out at the market.

"Twenty bucks our names aren't on the list," Bree muttered.

"No kidding." I looked at Lachlan. "Think you can freeze them?"

"Definitely. Then move fast."

"No need for the speed," Bree said. "You freeze them, I'll make us invisible."

"Perfect." We were a good team. "Lachlan will lead the way in, and we'll go single file after him."

Everyone nodded.

I didn't feel Lachlan's magic this time—no doubt, he was trying to hide his not-evil signature—but the guards froze in place. They didn't so much as twitch. If you weren't paying attention, though, you wouldn't even notice.

A half second later, my friends disappeared. I started for the door to the casino, bumping into someone slightly. One by one, we filed through the door, entering a dimmed lobby. There was a hostess standing at a gold-lined table, but she was frozen solid, too.

Well done, Lachlan.

"Everyone here?" I whispered.

There was a chorus of three yeses and one aye, and we all hurried past the hostess. As soon as we'd passed her, Bree and Lachlan dropped their magic. As a group, we strode right into the casino.

I tried to act like I belonged here, but the sheer opulence of the place made my jaw drop. Literally. It was embarrassing.

The whole place was done up in gold and gems and velvets. Many of the patrons wore cloaks like ours, but others were dressed in tuxes and ball gowns. Still others wore rougher clothes, but the waitresses seemed to be just as attentive to them.

In the casino, all money was green.

There were a half dozen games that I could spot off the bat, though I couldn't have identified them. All the tables were crowded full of people. We drifted toward one of the many bars set up along the edges of the huge room.

There were two more entrances that I could see, both toward the back.

"We should split up and guard the entrances," Lachlan said.

"You should hunt for the target, Ana," Bree said. "You're the ones who got us here. You and Lachlan take this one. The rest of us will guard the doors and keep an eye on you."

"Thanks, guys." I smiled at them.

They melted into the crowd, their cloaks disappearing between the tables.

"Let's go," Lachlan said.

I followed him out into the crowd, drifting between tables, pretending to look for a game to play. In reality, I was looking for a pale demon with blond hair and sawed-off horns. Normally, demons didn't look very human, but there were the rare exceptions.

The longer we walked, the more I felt the prickle of eyes on the back of my neck.

"You feel that?" I asked.

"Aye. Someone is watching."

"The guards?" I glanced around, spotting at least eight guards.

"They're looking for cheats. Not sure they're worried about us." Lachlan rubbed the back of his neck. "But someone is definitely watching."

My skin crawled as we searched, tension ratcheting up. Whenever I caught sight of my sisters or Caro, they looked alert, too. This place was definitely dangerous. For all the glitter and gleam that coated the surface of it, the underbelly was dark.

When a hand roughly grabbed my arm, I bit back a scream. My heart thundered. I couldn't start a scene, but if management had caught us...

We were screwed.

13

I glanced back, dread uncoiling in my stomach.

My friend Claire stared back at me, shock on her face. She wore a fabulous red dress and black stilettos. So much makeup covered her face that I barely recognized her. But it was definitely her.

"What are you doing here?" she asked. "You shouldn't be here."

"I know. What are *you* doing here?" And dressed like that? Normally, she only wore her fighting leathers or jeans and a T-shirt.

"Come on." She tugged my arm. "We need to get out of the crowd."

I followed her toward the edge of the casino, Lachlan at my back. Claire strode through the tables like she knew the place. But she wasn't a gambler. I sniffed.

Her magic smelled different. Like rotten meat and gasoline.

I gagged slightly.

What the hell was going on?

She pulled us to the edge of the gambling hall, right between two big potted trees. A bench sat pressed against the wall, a perfect place to get away from the crowd.

I looked at Lachlan. "Can you block the sound?"

He nodded.

Claire visibly relaxed. "No one can hear?"

"No one," Lachlan said. "You don't have to whisper."

"What the hell is going on?" I asked. "Does Connor know you're here?"

"My brother doesn't know everything," she said. "He wouldn't approve of this job."

"You're on a job?" I asked.

"Why the hell else would I be in a place like this, stinking like an old butcher shop right before an arsonist went to town?"

Okay, she had a point.

"I'm hunting a mob boss." She tapped the black diamond necklace that hung around her neck. "This makes me blend in, though. A bit like your cloak, but prettier."

"This place has a mob?" I asked.

She gave me a deadpan look. "It's a casino. Of course it has a mob."

"So the Order of the Magica knows about this place, then," Lachlan said.

"They do." Claire spent most of her time working as a free-lance mercenary and odd-jobs-woman for the Order of the Magica. "They don't want to take this place out entirely, but they do want to clean it up some."

"Why don't they want to take it out?" I asked.

"The Order's not all good," Claire said.

"That's the truth." They hunted FireSouls like Nix, and she certainly wasn't bad. They might be the government, and they might *try* to take care of most supernaturals, but they didn't always do a good job. They certainly didn't hesitate to let their prejudice run wild.

My gaze traveled from Claire back toward the crowd of gamblers, finally landing on a mop of messy blond hair. Two sawed-off horns stuck out.

I gasped. "That's him!"

She nodded. "I assumed you were looking for someone. Which one is it?"

I nodded toward the card table where the cards floated in midair, directed by a mage who acted as the dealer. "The blond demon. We've got to ask him some questions. Problem is, I don't know if he'll talk."

"Oh, he'll talk," Claire said. "You just got to get him into the Room of Truth."

"What's that?" Lachlan asked.

"This is the mob, right? So they've got to make people talk all the time. But regular old beatings don't work great for supernaturals. We're used to getting the shit beaten out of us. And often, we've got scary people on our tails anyway. So they've got a room that has been imbued with a truth charm. Get your guy in there, ask him some questions, and bam! You've got your answers."

"Perfect." I liked this plan. "But how do we get him in there?"

"We can't grab him, or people will be suspicious," Lachlan said.

"Pretend to comp him something," Claire said.

"Comp?"

"Give him something on behalf of the casino. He's got a major gambling problem. He'll go anywhere if you promise him credit or a better table."

I looked down at my cloak. "He's not going to follow me anywhere."

"We'll trade clothes," Claire said. "I'd do it for you, but he'll recognize me. I see him here all the time, and he knows I'm not staff. But I just arrived today, so he hasn't seen this dress. We'll trade clothes and stinky charms, and you lure him in."

"You're a lifesaver."

She grinned. "The boss isn't here tonight, so my plan was a bust anyway." She grabbed my hand and pulled me away from the wall. "We'll find a bathroom and get changed."

Ten minutes later, I teetered out of the bathroom on Claire's stiletto heels. We were the same size, but heels had not been a part of my life in...well, ever.

I liked them; I'd just never had time to wear them. It wasn't easy to run for your life in heels. Now I was suffering for that inexperience.

Before we'd gone to the bathroom, Claire had shown me where the Room of Truth was located, and I'd used my comms charm to alert the others. They'd act as guards, and once we'd gotten our target into the room, we'd make quick work of questioning him.

If Arach's heart really was for sale in this awful place, I didn't want to give anyone enough time to make an offer on it.

I turned the corner and met Lachlan's gaze. His eyes traveled halfway down my body, heating as he took in the tight dress. Warmth flowed through me. Then he stiffened, as if realizing what he was doing, and jerked his gaze to mine.

"You look lovely." His voice was slightly rough.

"Thanks." I passed him. "Meet me at the room?"

"I'll be there. Be safe."

"You too." I walked past him, heading out into the main room. I tried to put some swagger into my step and almost fell over.

Right. No swagger until I'd had more practice. Right now, I'd focus on getting to the demon's table in one piece.

But when I neared the table, I realized he wasn't there.

Crap.

I spun in a circle, heart thundering. He had to be here.

Finally, my gaze landed on the bar on the side of the room. My target stood there, leaning over the gleaming wood and trying to get the bartender's attention. I walked toward him, choosing the empty spot to his left.

My heart thundered as I got ready for my charade, hoping that he'd buy it.

"Excuse me, Mr. Karth?" Claire had told me his name, and I tried to keep my voice pleasantly modulated, channeling a fancy woman at a salon. I'd never *been* to a salon, but those ladies had always struck me as the height of fancy.

He turned, his gaze raking up and down my body. *This* felt nothing like Lachlan's warm gaze, and I tried to control the shudder. Karth had the aura of a snake-oil salesman. "What's up, pretty lady?"

Ew. "Management would like me to guide you to a special table. You've been such a loyal customer that they want to upgrade you."

He grinned, tugging on his red jacket. The slime practically oozed off of him. "Why, that's mighty kind of them. Do you come with the deal?"

Double ew. I flattened my features and forced my mouth to move. "Perhaps we can arrange something."

The words almost made me gag, but they did get him to follow me. My heart pounded as I led him from the main casino floor to the hallway.

"What's this now?" he asked.

"The table isn't on the main floor. Our highest rollers don't gamble there."

"I wouldn't call myself a high roller." Nerves echoed in his voice.

"Oh, but you will be."

His eyes brightened at that.

Moron.

I picked up the pace, my heels clacking on the tile floor. There was no one in this part of the hall, but it was still opulently decorated, so he shouldn't be suspicious. Yet.

When his hand landed on my butt, I almost elbowed him in the nose. My arm twitched, and it took everything I had not to crush his face. I clenched my teeth and sucked in a deep breath. With a shaking hand, I gripped his wrist gently and removed it.

"Later." I smiled, knowing it looked more like a dog baring its teeth, but he didn't seem to notice. Mostly because his gaze was glued to my butt.

Ick.

It reminded me of my job waitressing back in Death Valley, before we'd gotten the buggy up and running. I'd been *real* determined to find any work besides that.

Near the end of the hall, I turned toward a large wooden door that gleamed in the light, pushing it open and leading him inside.

This was where it would get tricky, since this hallway had way less frills. Anyone with a clue in their head would realize that the high rollers wouldn't be gambling in a room that was connected to a hallway as ugly as this one.

But Karth, the Moron, had eyes only for my ass, so he followed me in. We were a full ten feet down the hall before he noticed that the environment had changed substantially.

"Hey, what is this place?" he demanded.

"We're nearly there."

"But—" He grabbed my arm.

I spun and punched him in the throat, having no more patience for this shit. We were out of the public spaces, anyway.

Karth gasped, and his eyes bugged out. He gripped his throat, betrayal flashing in his gaze.

What did he expect from the woman whose ass he had grabbed?

"You're a moron, Karth," I said.

His face twisted, and he reached for me.

Lachlan appeared through a doorway. He was on Karth in seconds, dragging the guy away from me.

"Hey, he was mine!" I said.

"Don't play with your prey." He grinned at me. "Anyway, I don't think his ego could handle being beaten by a woman."

"I don't care what his ego can handle." I glared at Karth, who was currently shrieking his head off. No sound came out, though, no doubt due to Lachlan's magic. "Let's go."

Lachlan dragged Karth down the hall.

Bree peeked her head out of a door, then grinned. "Come on."

I hurried into the room, shivering as the magic washed over me.

Oh boy. Lachlan had better not ask me how I really felt about him while I was in here, or I was going to embarrass myself.

Lachlan threw Karth into the chair in the middle of the room. Bree was the only one here besides us.

"The others are on guard," she said.

"Perfect." I turned toward Karth. Lachlan gripped his shoulders, keeping his butt pressed down into the chair. My target's face was a mottled red as he spat words at me. I was sure they were insults, but I still couldn't hear him. "All right, Karth. You're going to tell us who you sold Arach's heart to."

Lachlan's magic lifted.

"You bitch!"

"I am." I smiled sweetly. "Tell me who you sold Arach's heart to."

His mouth twisted, as if he were trying to keep the words in, then he spat. "Didn't sell it."

"You didn't?"

"No."

"What'd you do with it, then?" I asked.

"Delivered it to the Extractor."

"Who is that?"

He shrugged, a dumb look crossing his face. "The Extractor. I don't know who she is, other than that she's called the Extractor."

"That's a weird name. Does she wear a brown cloak?"

"No."

"Do you know someone who wears a long brown cloak?"

"No."

Hmm. I wonder if the cloaked figure had used an intermediary to hire Karth. Probably.

"Where is the Extractor?" I asked.

His face twisted, but finally, he spit the words out. "She's got a shop here in Grimrealm. Other side of the main market. It's named after her."

Okay, this was good. We were really getting somewhere. "Who hired you to do this?"

He snapped his mouth shut, desperate not to speak.

"Come on, who hired you?"

"It was—"

"Incoming!" The comms charm at my neck blared to life. "Three demon guards, headed your way."

My gaze darted to the door. It burst open, and three massive demons charged in. Each had the dark red skin of a fire demon, and their suits bulged with muscles. Large black horns extended from their heads, each decorated with silver spikes.

In unison, they hurled blasts of flame at the three of us. I was standing close to Bree, and I threw out my shield, blocking both of us.

It flickered briefly, almost failing to appear, then it burst to life, forming a white barrier that protected us from the flame. The fire crashed into it, making my arms shake, but the barrier held strong.

Karth wasn't so lucky. The blast slammed right into him. Lachlan, who'd been standing behind him, lunged backward, avoiding the worst of the blow.

Karth lit up like a torch, but his screams were silent. Lachlan blocked them, thank fates, hopefully buying us some time before more guards were alerted to the scene. I'd have felt bad for Karth if he hadn't been the one to steal Arach's heart.

We had two seconds max before the fire demons recharged.

I drew my dagger from the ether, then dropped my shield and threw the blade at the nearest demon. It thudded into his neck, and he keeled over backward.

Bree drew her sword, lunging for a second attacker. Lachlan was fast. One second, he stood there as a man. Magic swirled around him, flashing bright, then he was a black lion, leaping toward the third demon. His long claws swiped across the demon's throat, sending blood flying.

The demon collapsed. Bree's opponent thudded to the ground, missing a head.

In a flash of light, Lachlan shifted back to human. He turned to our target, then sighed, clearly disappointed. "Questioning is over."

Karth was nothing but ash. He'd be waking up back in hell soon.

"We need to get out of here." I knelt by the nearest demon and searched his pockets.

Bree did the same. I came up empty, but she held up her hand. "Jackpot! Transport charm."

"Perfect." I stood.

Lachlan checked the last demon, but he, too, came up empty.

"At least we have a clue." I sidled up to the door and peeked out.

At the end of the hall, Claire gestured wildly. She'd used magic to change her hair to red, but I'd recognize her anywhere.

"Come on, guys," I said.

We sprinted down the hall toward them. Rowan and Caro waited with her, and Claire led us on a twisty route through the back of the casino.

"If you took out the demons, you should have a bit of a head start," she whispered.

"What about you?"

"I don't think my cover is blown. No one has seen me back here, and I was only on the main floor for a minute." She led us to a door. Next to it, a man slumped against the wall, asleep. No doubt courtesy of Claire. She pushed open the door, revealing an alley, then slipped outside.

We followed.

"Guard us while we change," Claire said.

My friends stood with their backs to us while Claire and I stripped, trading clothes.

"You sure you're okay?" I asked her.

"Fine. Don't worry about me." She pointed to her head. "The hair glamour helps. I'll be okay."

Claire was a pro, so I trusted her. You didn't live long as a mercenary without knowing your way around a sticky situation.

"Did you get what you needed?" she asked.

"We have to go to the Extractor. Do you know who that is?"

She shook her head. "I've heard of her, but I don't know what she does. She's expensive, and only works with the worst of the worst." She looked around, shrugging. "Which pretty much goes for everyone in this hellhole."

"Be careful, okay?" Bree said.

"Always. You too." She saluted. "I've got to get back in now. Pretend to act normal and all that. And wake up the guard."

"Thanks for the help," I said.

"Anytime. Come by P & P to tell me what happens." She hurried back through the door.

I tugged the cloak up over my head, cringing at the feeling of spiders skittering over my skin, then turned to my friends. "Ready?"

"Let's do this," Rowan said.

We hurried out of the alley and into the market, pushing our way through the crowds that heaved between the stalls. As Karth had directed, we headed straight toward the other side of the market. A few minutes of searching led us down a narrow alley, where there was a simple black door with the words *The Extractor* written on it.

A man stood out front, his green top hat tipped jauntily on his head.

"Can I help you?" His voice carried a sibilant hiss.

"We're here to see the Extractor," Lachlan said.

"I'm certain you're not," he said.

"We are." I stepped forward. "I'm *certain* I'd know our intentions."

"Be that as it may, she does not have an appointment with five cloaked figures today."

That was fair. And smart. Because I was probably going to try to kill this woman, if she was messing around with Arach's heart.

Lachlan raised his hand a few inches, clearly about to freeze the guy in his tracks. But the doorman was too fast. Magic swirled around him, and a half second later, he transformed into a giant snake.

He lunged at Lachlan, knocking him off his feet, then wrapped around me like a giant boa constrictor. I gasped, my air totally cut off.

Bree leapt forward, swinging her sword for the snake's head. She sliced it right off, and it thudded to the ground. But the body stayed wrapped around me, slowly crushing my muscles and bones. I tried to suck in air, my vision fading, but nothing entered my lungs.

Lachlan lunged upward, grabbing the snake around the middle. He heaved, veins standing out at his neck, and pulled the snake off of me. The beast uncoiled, then flopped to the ground.

Gasping, I stumbled away and choked out a word: "Thanks."

Lachlan nodded, searching the area around us. "I don't think anyone saw."

He was right. The alley was suitably dark and abandoned. "Let's get inside, then."

Lachlan pulled open the door, and the five of us hurried in. The shop within was entirely unassuming. It was a medium-sized space with shelves cluttered full of objects. Honestly, it looked a bit like Ancient Magic, except for the fact that it was dripping with dark magic and made my skin crawl.

I shuddered at the feel of the place. It was just as bad as my cloak, if not worse. This whole underground area stank of evil and desperation. No wonder Aerdeca and Mordaca had left and refused to return.

I stepped a few feet into the space.

A man wearing another green top hat entered the room from a door at the back. "Can I help you?"

"We're looking for the Extractor," Lachlan said.

I stiffened as a sense of familiar magic washed over me. It

was coming from the door behind the man. I stepped closer, desperate to get another hit of that magic.

"She is not in, I'm afraid." The man eyed us warily. "Sibbie let you in?"

I had to assume that was the doorman. I stepped closer and nodded absently. "He let us in."

What is that magic?

I took another step forward, getting a stronger hit of the magic. I nearly stumbled backward, gasping. "Arach."

"What?" Bree's voice was sharp from behind me.

I pointed to the door behind the man. "There."

Then I sprinted full out, determined to get to her. Arach's heart was back there. I could feel her magic, crashing over me in waves. I'd never forget that feeling.

"Stop!" The man lunged for us.

My friends raced after me.

"Master!" the man shouted, right before he turned into a giant snake. He shot for us, his long fangs glinting in the light. Venom dripped off them, green and shiny.

"I've got this!" Rowan hurtled past me, sword raised. She sliced off the snake's head before it reached her, then dived away from the body.

We sprinted around the remains, then straight through the door that would lead us to Arach's heart.

As soon as I entered, I skidded to a halt, horror opening up a well inside of me. "Holy fates."

I'd never seen anything like it.

A mad scientist's lair, complete with a pit full of snakes.

14

"Holy fates, what *is* this place?" Bree muttered.

I studied the huge space, which dipped down like a perfect round amphitheater. At the bottom, in the middle, Arach's heart was hooked up to some kind of crazy contraption that shot light straight into it. It was suspended over a basin of some kind, but I had no idea what the purpose was.

Wide steps led down to the heart, but each was covered with massive snakes. They writhed, guarding their contraption. Overhead, lightning struck, making the room glow eerily. The noise was thunderous, echoing off the walls.

Bree raised her hands, her magic surging.

It was clear that she was trying to call upon the lightning, a gift from Thor, Norse god of lightning.

Her brow creased as she focused. The lightning struck, a dozen bolts heading straight for the snakes. It lit them up, and they writhed, twisting around in the amphitheater pit. They lunged toward the lightning bolts, drinking it up.

"Holy fates, they *like* it," Rowan said.

Oh crap. She was right.

The lightning seemed to be feeding the snakes.

Bree let her hands fall. "Well, forget that."

She dragged off her disgusting cloak, letting her wings flare wide. They gleamed silver and bright. She shot into the air, flying over the pit of snakes, headed right for Arach's heart.

She was going to get it!

Then one of the snakes lunged out of the pit, leaping for her. It flew through the air, over twenty feet high, performing a feat of acrobatics that should have been impossible for an animal without legs.

What the heck?

What kind of dark magic made *that* possible?

Right before Bree reached Arach's heart, the snake's head plowed into her. She screamed, flying through the air and landing with a thud on the pile of serpents.

Lachlan leapt forward, throwing out his hands and freezing them. "I can't hold it long!"

Bree scrambled to her feet, drawing her sword from the ether. Her silver wings looked bent and broken, the fall having crushed them beneath her weight. "I can't fly, but I can fight!"

Three tiny blurs streaked by me, racing for the snakes.

"The cats!" Rowan cried.

She was right.

Somehow the Cats of Catastrophe had appeared! They had a knack for waiting until I really needed them, and now was definitely the time.

Muffin, Bojangles, and Princess Snowflake III leapt into the pit of snakes.

"What are you doing?!" a voice shouted.

My gaze darted from the snakes to the edge of the amphitheater. On the other side, an irate woman was charging toward us. She wore a vibrant green dress that looked like snake scales, and her hair was a silver cloud. Manic light gleamed in her eyes, and the scent of her magic was dry and reptilian.

"The Extractor," Caro said. "I'll take care of her."

She raced for the woman, sprinting around the side of the amphitheater.

I charged after the Cats of Catastrophe, Rowan at my side. As I neared the first step down, Lachlan's magic faded.

"That's all I've got!" he shouted.

The snakes burst to life, writhing and slithering.

I leapt down onto the first stair, joining Muffin, who was going for the eyes of one of the great beasts. I stabbed one in the neck with my sword. It hissed wildly, then exploded in a burst of black dust.

They were magic! Not real.

Good.

I preferred destroying magic rather than animals.

I lunged for another, leading with my sword.

Lachlan hurtled past me in his lion form, ripping and tearing at any snake that got in his way. He cleared a path, so I followed, passing by Princess Snowflake III, who was coated in the black snake dust. She leapt onto another serpent, Bojangles following close behind her.

I darted past one attacking snake, but was stopped by a second. It was too quick, wrapping itself around my middle before I could stab it with my sword.

"Lachlan!" I cried.

He spun around, hurtling back toward me on enormous paws. His massive jaws sank into the snake's side, and he yanked, pulling the creature off of me.

Panting, I ran past him, nearly to the platform at the bottom of the amphitheater. Arach's heart called to me, the magic crashing over me in waves that seemed to give me strength and speed. I darted around one and stabbed another in the throat, narrowly avoiding the sharp fangs that headed straight for my shoulder.

On the opposite side of the amphitheater, Bree battled her way toward Arach's heart. Above her, Caro fought the Extractor, who whipped out at her with her tremendously long arms.

Holy fates! The woman had snakes for arms.

Caro beat them back with concentrated jets of water, holding her own. With one enormous blast, she took out the Extractor altogether, sending the woman flying back a dozen feet.

Caro laughed, her hood thrown back from her head to reveal her shiny platinum head, then dived into the pit of snakes, ready to keep fighting.

I beat my way past one last serpent, then stumbled onto the platform where Arach's heart was hooked up to the crazy contraption.

A sharp beam of light was shooting straight into the stone heart, fueled by the lightning from above. A single drop of pearly blue liquid dripped from the bottom of the heart into a basin below.

Those bastards!

I didn't know what they were trying to do with her heart, but I knew it was bad freaking news.

I touched the stone heart, the light sending shockwaves of pain through my hands and arms. Tears sprang to my eyes at the unbelievable burning sensation, but I gripped Arach's heart and yanked it out of the light, stumbling backward.

Magic burst out from the heart, some kind of unfamiliar spell igniting at my touch.

What the hell?

In the distance, a roar sounded.

I glanced up.

The cloaked figure!

He'd just appeared, no doubt called by the spell that I'd just ignited when I grabbed the heart.

"Ana!" Bree shouted.

She'd fought her way down to the platform and stood on the other side, about fifteen feet away from me.

"Bree! Get this thing out of here! Use the charm!" I threw the heart at her, and she lunged, snagging it out of the air. "Go!"

She didn't hesitate, just dug into her pocket and grabbed the transport charm she'd stolen from the demon, then chucked it on the ground. She lunged into the portal, taking the heart with her.

To safety.

The cloaked figure roared, a sound of rage unlike any I'd ever heard.

"It's gone!" I screamed. "You lose!"

I sprinted for him, realizing that the snakes were racing away in the other direction, desperate to escape him. Lachlan, Rowan, and Caro joined me.

Together, we ran for the cloaked figure, sprinting up the stairs, dodging the fleeing snakes. We neared him at the same time, slamming into a force field that held us tight. Frozen.

Then the ether sucked us in, tearing us away from the Extractor's lair. My head spun as I rocketed through space, heading toward the unknown.

When the ether spit me out into the darkness, I fell to my knees, gasping.

Heart thundering, I scrambled upright. We were in a field that smelled of wheat, and the night was cool and dark.

"Where the hell are we?" I asked.

"No idea," Rowan said.

But the cloaked figure had brought us here. My friends stumbled to their feet. The cloaked figure raised its hands, sending out a blast of magic so strong that it sent me flying off my feet. I smashed into the ground about ten yards away, my insides feeling like they'd been pulverized.

It was magic like Bree's sonic boom, but instead of being one direct hit, the blast had radiated out from the cloaked figure in a complete circle, taking out every one of us.

My skin chilled. That was new. And *powerful.*

I staggered to my feet, my muscles shaking.

Beside me, Caro raised her hands, shooting the cloaked figure with a blast of water the size of a semi-truck. Thousands of gallons shot toward the figure, slamming into him and throwing him back.

Caro stumbled to her knees, her face white. She gasped. "I'm tapped out."

Rowan charged, her blade raised. She was closest, and she reached our enemy as soon as he stood. Rowan swung her blade, aiming for the head, but the cloaked figure threw out a hand. Magic hurtled toward her and slammed into her chest.

Rowan spun in a circle, flying away and crashing to the ground. I raced for the figure, but Lachlan beat me to him. He was so fast in his lion form. He jumped into the air and landed on the figure, throwing him back onto the ground.

They wrestled, each equivalently strong. Magic swelled around the figure. A sonic boom exploded out from him, throwing Lachlan off of him. The lion flew through the air, then landed with such a crash that the ground shook.

The figure lunged toward Rowan, who was slowly rising from the ground.

I charged, grabbing the figure's cloak, trying to slow his momentum toward my sister.

Dark magic shivered up my arm, making my stomach turn and my muscles quiver. I gritted my teeth and yanked, calling on my magic—any magic—to help me. The light that was deep inside me flared to life, and I begged it to rise to the surface, imagining using it to save Rowan. To save us all.

The magic burst forth, a sharp white light that blinded even me.

A terrible shriek sounded, coming from the figure whose cloak I gripped. I pulled harder. As my vision cleared, the cloak ripped away, as if I'd loosened it from the wearer.

Three ghostly figures exploded forth, shooting for the sky.

I tumbled backward, the cloak gripped in my hand.

The three ghosts—or phantoms or wraiths or *something*—shot away so fast that I barely got a look at them. There were three, maybe female, and then they were gone.

Panting, I dropped the cloak, then stumbled to my feet.

Rowan finally managed to rise, her face pale and her limbs shaking. Caro wasn't much better off, but at least she was standing. But Lachlan...

He lay sprawled on the ground in his human form. He'd been hit with a direct shot from the cloaked figure.

Panic thundered through me.

I sprinted for him and fell to my knees at his side.

His face was white, his form still.

I'd never seen anyone take such a hit from so close. I touched his chest, tears pricking at my eyes. "Lachlan!"

He didn't move.

I couldn't breathe as I shook him, trying to wake him up. "Lachlan?"

His eyes opened, stark in his pale face. They zeroed in on me. Confusion gave way to recognition and something I couldn't identify.

He touched my cheek. His voice was rough as he said, "I don't want to wait anymore."

"Wait?"

"For you. Pretending there's nothing here is stupid."

"You nearly died, and that was your big realization."

"It seemed good enough to me. I—"

"Guys!" Rowan's panicked voice cut through the night. "Incoming!"

I didn't want to look away from Lachlan—not when he was saying things like this—but Rowan's tone made it clear that shit was about to hit the fan.

I surged to my feet as a roar sounded in the distance. I turned, catching sight of an army of demons thundering toward us. They were armed to the teeth, their gazes bright on us.

I looked at Lachlan, who was climbing to his feet, still shaky from the blow.

"I've got it." His voice was strained, but he held up his hand, creating a portal to get us the hell out of here.

It took a moment—his magic was nearly tapped out—but finally, it flared to life. One by one, we leapt in, just as the demons got within shooting range.

We arrived back at the Protectorate, panting and high on adrenaline. I'd grabbed the discarded cloak before jumping into the portal, though it was doubtful that it would provide any answers now that the three figures weren't wearing it.

We appeared at the edge of the courtyard. As usual, the air was cool and damp in the Highlands. The moon shined high in the sky, illuminating the castle with a pale white glow. We yanked off our horrible cloaks, and I breathed a sigh of relief to feel the dark magic no longer touching my skin.

"Can't wait to destroy these things," Rowan muttered.

"Ditto." Caro nodded.

"What the hell was that thing that flew out of the cloak?" Rowan asked.

"I have no idea." I looked toward the dark sky, as if I might see it here, at the castle. "But I doubt that's the last we'll see of it."

As if they'd heard us arrive, Ali and Haris pushed open the main doors and ran out.

"Are you okay?" Ali shouted.

"Everyone safe?" Haris added.

"We're fine!" Caro yelled.

"Is Bree back?" I ran toward them, my friends at my side.

"She's back! And the ghosts are doing better." Ali grinned widely. "It looks like you did it."

I glanced at Lachlan, who looked stronger now. There were so many things I wanted to say to him, but Arach and the ghosts had to come first. He nodded, as if he understood.

I sprinted into the entry hall, pulling to a stop when I spotted the Pugs of Destruction, racing down the stairs like their tails were on fire. They were no longer faded and weak, but just as vibrant as they'd ever been.

Mayhem flew right toward us, her tongue lolling out of her mouth. Right before she reached us, she farted fire, then spun in a circle, clearly confused.

I laughed. "Oh, thank fates."

Bree ran down the stairs after them, a huge smile on her face. "Are you all right? Is anyone injured?"

"We're fine," I said. "Just beat-up."

Every muscle ached, and I was sure my friends felt like crap, too. But we were all walking, which meant we were doing dandy.

The Cats of Catastrophe appeared in the hall, each coated with the black snake dust. They spotted the pugs and meowed, then chased them back up the stairs, the six of them going on a rampage through the upstairs corridor that would definitely piss off Potts. I grinned.

"Where is Arach?" Lachlan asked.

"In her office." Bree gestured for us to follow her down the hall. "Let's go find her. Jude is with her."

I sucked in a deep breath. *Jude.* We'd succeeded, so I was sure Jude would be happy with me.

Well, I was pretty sure.

Whatever the case, I wanted her to be *really* happy. Same for the rest of the directors. Happy enough to cut me some slack on blowing Lavender off her feet and to maybe advance me another level at the Academy.

As a group, we hurried down the hall. Lachlan stayed near my side as Bree led us into Arach's colorful office, the tall walls covered with bright paintings.

Arach stood next to the fire, glowing brilliantly. Florian stood next to her, looking just as good. He was no longer pale and wispy, thank fates, and his tall, curling wig sat proudly on his head.

Jude, Hedy, and the rest of the department heads stood at their sides. Everyone turned to face us. Florian shot us a massive smile.

"Are you all right?" Jude demanded.

"We're fine," Lachlan said.

Jude's face relaxed. "Good. And well done."

I strode over to Arach, inspecting her. She looked normal. "Are you better?"

"Much." She nodded, a serene smile on her face. "But tell us what you learned."

"All right."

We all took a seat around the table in the middle of the room.

Lachlan looked at me, holding my gaze for a moment. "I think this is Ana's story to tell. She called the shots."

"And made good calls," Caro said.

I smiled at her.

Bree nodded enthusiastically, though she didn't bother to speak on my behalf. We all knew that she was so biased in my favor that I could have spent the whole adventure burping and falling, and she'd have said I did pretty good.

"Can't say that I'm surprised you did well!" Florian said. "An exemplary trainee!"

I smiled at him, glad to have one person—ghost—in my corner.

"What happened?" Jude asked. "What did you learn?"

I explained our trip through Grimrealm, and about finding Arach's heart hooked up to the strange contraption in the middle of the snake pit.

Arach frowned, touching her chest. Her heart might not be in there anymore—it was deep below the castle again, I had to imagine—but still, I couldn't blame her for being weirded out.

I leaned forward. "Once I touched the heart, it activated some kind of spell that alerted the cloaked figure. He—they— appeared immediately. We all ran for the figure, but as soon as we reached it, some kind of spell ignited and swept us away."

"To be clear, the cloaked figure took you away?" Jude asked.

"I think so." I shook my head. "It didn't want us to be in that room anymore. Once Arach's heart was gone, it took us right out of there."

"But why? Surely, it might have had backup where you were?" Hedy asked.

"It took us to a field, where we fought. Eventually, we drove the cloaked figure away. Then reinforcements showed up."

"So the figure took you there to get rid of you?" Jude said. "It had backup in that field."

"I think so, though it took them time to make their way to us. I don't think the cloaked figure expected to run into us when it appeared at the Extractor's lair."

"It would never expect us to make it into Grimrealm at all," Lachlan said.

I thought back to Arach's heart. "I don't think the cloaked

figure took us away just to kill us. I think it didn't want us getting whatever was in the basin under the heart."

"What do you mean?" Hedy asked.

I explained the single glowing droplet that had fallen from the heart, keeping my gaze on Arach.

She nodded. "I am not surprised. I feel slightly weaker than I was before. Not much, but something is missing."

"The Extractor," Lachlan said. "He took something from your heart. Magic."

"I think so." Arach nodded. "I don't know if they got all that they needed, but it sounds like the cloaked figure didn't want you to get whatever they had taken."

"And now it's long gone," Bree said. "No way they didn't move it right away."

"I have to agree on that point," Jude said. "But we can send in backup to check."

"We can go," I said.

She pointed at me. "*You* need to rest. Ali and Haris can go, along with reinforcements. If you tell them how to get there, they'll have no problem. My instinct is that it's pointless recon, anyway, but we have to try."

She was right. I was way too beat, and it was probably pointless.

"So the cloaked figure was the mastermind," Jude said. "But you have no idea who it was?"

"Three wraiths," I said. "Or ghosts. I couldn't make out much."

"I think they were women," Bree added.

"Their magic was powerful." Caro shivered. "If Ana hadn't yanked their cloak off, we'd have been done for."

"It must have bound them to the physical plane," Hedy said. "I've heard of such things."

"So they're ghosts?" I asked.

She shrugged. "Hard to say. But how did you get the cloak off? That should be impossible."

"My magic. Lachlan has been helping me, and I used my new light power against them. It helped me tear the cloak off them."

"Perhaps you're connected to them, somehow," Jude said.

I didn't like the sound of that. But I couldn't deny it. Lachlan had wrestled with them in lion form, and even he hadn't managed to get it off them.

"We'll get to the bottom of it," Jude said. "In the meantime, well done, Ana. You broke the rules, but you delivered."

"Thank you."

"I think that calls for some celebration." She grinned. "You've advanced another level at the Academy."

15

After we finished the meeting and everyone began to disperse, Lachlan grabbed my hand and pulled me into an abandoned nook in the hallway, tucking us behind a statue, deep in the shadows.

I'd been stealing looks at him through the meeting, but this was the first time we'd had even a second to ourselves.

In this tiny space, I was standing so close to him that I could feel his heat. I shivered, anticipation and fear racing through me.

"Did you mean it?" I demanded.

His dark gaze met mine. "I did."

"Why? What made you change your mind?"

His eyes were serious. "Two things. My heart stopped briefly when the cloaked figure hit me with the sonic boom." He reached for my hand. My heart thudded as his strong grip closed over my palm. "I realized that I was being an idiot. I won't live forever, and pretending that there's nothing here is stupid. Waiting to see if this goes away is stupid."

"It's not going away." I hadn't been able to stop thinking about him, even when I knew I shouldn't be.

"I know. I had my reasons, but they were shite."

"What reasons? And what was the second thing that changed your mind?" The words spilled out of me.

"When I was in the Room of Truth, I realized that I wanted you more than anything. It was simple, really."

Warmth exploded in my chest. *He wanted me more than anything.* It was the nicest thing a guy had ever said to me. I smiled so big I could feel it. "Same. I didn't want you to ask me what I was thinking, or I'd be forced into telling the truth."

"I'm sorry I was an idiot," he said. "But I don't want to be one anymore."

This was great. But I wasn't about to let him off the hook so easy. *I* hadn't been the one to delay this unnecessarily.

I looked him up and down. "Well, maybe you were too big of an idiot and waited too long."

The corner of his lips hiked up in a sexy smile. "Not going to let me off the hook easy, are you?"

"You're going to have to earn your way into my good graces." I crossed my arms. "It's going to take a lot of hard work."

"Is it, then?"

"Aye." I mimicked his brogue. "What's your plan?"

"I was thinking we'd start with a kiss."

"Really? Because I was thinking you should wash my car." I pursed my lips, pretending to consider his suggestion. "But if the kiss was a good one…"

He gripped my waist and pulled me toward him, making my heart leap. His smile faded into an intense expression as he dipped his head toward mine. His lips captured mine in an expert kiss, and all rational thought fled.

I melted into him, swept away by the sensation. He groaned, wrapping his strong arms around me. Every inch of his body was hot and hard. I wanted to touch all of him, and I kissed him as if my life depended on it.

"Ana!"

Bree's voice tore me from the kiss. I jerked my head away.

"Lachlan!" Jude's voice echoed down the hall.

Fates.

I looked at Lachlan, eyes wide.

"Jude wants to speak with me."

"And Bree." I'd promised her I'd go to the Whisky and Warlock. Crap.

"We'll finish this later," Lachlan said.

"I'm counting on it." I moved to dart away.

He grabbed my arm, pulling me back. With a grin, he said, "And I will wash your car."

As usual, we ended up at the Whisky and Warlock for our celebration. I was tired, but not too tired to get some food and a drink with my friends. Lachlan had stayed behind to speak with Jude, and I'd be lying if I said I hadn't wished he'd come with us.

It wasn't until I walked in the pub door that I realized he hadn't told me his reasons for delaying things between us. He'd said he had them, but I'd been so distracted by the *I want you more than anything* comment that it'd completely slipped my mind.

I made a mental not to ask when I saw him again. Even without him here, it was still loads of fun. It was a celebration, after all. I'd mastered some of my magic and saved Arach's heart. She, Florian, and the pugs were all safe. So was the Protectorate. The institution needed Arach's magic just like she did. They were going to fill in the tunnel and put guards on the heart.

Muffin led the way into the pub, sauntering right up to the seat where Miss Kitty sat by the fire. The little black cat stared at him, unimpressed.

Clearly, Muffin was going to have to work for her affection.

Princess Snowflake III and Bojangles went straight for a back door that led to the kitchen, which didn't surprise me. The rest of us headed toward Sophie at the bar.

Today, her shirt read *Kiss My Haggis*. She grinned at us while wiping down the bar. "Good to see your lovely faces. What'll it be?"

Bree, Rowan, and Caro placed their orders, then Sophie shot me a grin as she pulled a bottle of cheap pink champagne out of the fridge. "I don't need to ask what you want."

"Nope!" I grinned and took the glass. "Thanks. It really goes fabulously with fish and chips."

"I'll have to take your word for it, but I'll put in an order."

"Me too!" There was a chorus from my friends.

Sophie grinned. "No problem. Your usual seats are waiting for you."

We found our table by the fire. As I lowered myself to the seat, every muscle in my body ached. As soon as my butt hit the wooden chair, I nearly melted into it. The fire warmed my back, and music played over the speakers.

This was amazing.

"Why does champagne always taste better after you kick some demon butt?" I asked.

"I don't know, but it does." Bree laughed and sipped her pink cocktail.

The pub was pretty full for a weeknight. At least, our section was. We were too far from the entrance to this room to see if the rest of the pub was heaving, but there were a lot of Protectorate members in here.

I spotted Lavender on the other side of the room, sitting with Angus and a few other classmates. She noticed me looking, and glanced away. Her hair was different. A wig, probably, since my magic had somehow singed hers off.

I frowned.

Bree caught my eye. "What's up?"

I nodded my head toward the other side of the room and whispered, "Lavender."

Bree scowled.

I chewed my lip, debating. But all I could see was her sprawled out on the floor of the training room, unconscious. Guilt tugged at me.

"I'm going to go say something to her." I stood.

"Don't start a fight," Rowan said.

"I'm not going to."

"Then what's the point of going over?" Bree asked.

"I want to apologize."

"What?" Bree's jaw dropped. "You heard the things she said about you. And she totally guns for you in class."

"I know. But I knocked her unconscious. She hasn't done that to me. And she's going to be my colleague one day. I can't help that she's kind of a bitch, but I can help what *I* do. And I'm going to apologize for knocking her out."

Bree frowned, clearly not liking what I was saying, then she sighed and smiled. "You're right. Go and be a bigger person. You were always nicer than me."

"I'd be ruthless if she picked on you, too," I said. "It's just that it's easier to shrug it off when it's me."

She nodded, and Rowan joined in. I grinned. It didn't matter if Lavender threw her beer in my face. I had my sisters.

I turned and headed toward her.

By the time I reached Lavender's table, I was definitely dragging my feet. She looked up as I stopped in front of her. Angus and the other two also looked up, their eyes widening.

"What do you want?" Lavender demanded.

"Just wanted to say sorry for knocking you unconscious."

"Oh. Okay. Thanks." She nodded and almost smiled. Then

her eyes narrowed in on my glass of pink champagne. She frowned. "That's not real champagne, you know. Real champagne is made in in France in a particular region. And that's *not* it."

Aaand that was the Lavender I knew. I laughed. "I will keep that in mind." I grinned and saluted. "But you have a good night."

I turned and walked back to my table.

"That didn't take long," Rowan said.

"It was as long as I could manage."

"Feel better?" Bree asked.

"Much. The air is better on the high road."

They laughed.

Rowan raised her glass in cheers. "To Ana, who can kick demon ass and apologize with the best of them."

"To Ana," they echoed.

I sat down and sipped my champagne, grateful to be with my friends. Life was good.

Exhaustion made me leave the Whisky and Warlock early. The rest of the gang was on their second drink, but I needed a nap. For twelve hours.

Muffin escorted me back through the portal and the enchanted forest, his green eyes gleaming in the dark.

"Did you strike out with Kitty?" I asked.

Good things are worth waiting for.

"Well, that's very...romantic." My cat was a romantic. Who'd have thought it?

He ignored me, of course.

The night air was chilly as we walked, bringing with it the scent of the sea and the sound of crashing waves. In the distance, the castle windows gleamed with golden lights. I grinned.

I'd saved Arach. I'd mastered some of my magic. And I was earning my place here.

All in all, not a bad day's work. Maybe I actually *could* handle this.

We crossed the lawn toward the castle, and I caught sight of the circle of stones that sat near the cliffs. The rocks rose tall toward the moon, silent sentinels that guarded the empty circle.

The fortune teller's words whispered in my head.

Answers.

The stone circle tugged at me.

I tried to ignore it, quickening my pace toward home. I wanted to see if Lachlan was still there. Maybe his meeting with Jude had run long.

But no matter how much I tried to ignore the stones, they pulled harder. There were answers there. I just knew it. They were dangerous answers, if my mother was to be believed, but I *needed* to know.

Not knowing was killing me.

I could handle it. I *had* to handle it.

I veered off toward the circle.

Muffin meowed. *What are you doing?*

"Looking for answers."

Finally.

He followed me toward the stones. Their pull grew as I neared. My heart began to pound.

I reached the first stone, a towering block of granite that rose twenty feet in the air. I pressed a hand to it, hesitating at the edge.

The circle tugged again, so hard that it dragged me across the boundary and into the empty space within.

Magic swept through me, lighting me up like a live wire. I

fell to my knees, gasping. Images flashed in my mind. Figures in white cloaks standing around a small, bent tree. Ancient writing carved in stones. A crashing sea.

And two words.

The Druid.

Muffin yowled. Something tugged at the back of my jacket, dragging me out of the stone circle. I passed the boundary of the stones, and the magic faded from me.

Gasping, I lay on the ground. My head spun, the stars whizzing by overhead.

Muffin meowed. *Idiot.*

My head reeled as I sat up.

Muffin stared at me. He'd dragged me out of the circle.

"Did you do that to protect me?"

Duh.

My upper arms burned and my mind buzzed. Frowning, I pulled off my jacket. My sleeves were burned away, and my upper arms were covered in scrolled, golden tattoos.

"What the hell?" I muttered.

Then a memory flashed. The words that I'd heard in the circle.

The Druid.

I was the Druid.

And that was dangerous.

THANK YOU FOR READING!

I hope you enjoyed Ana's first book as much as I enjoyed writing it. Reviews are *so* helpful to authors. If you want to leave one, you can do so on Amazon or GoodReads

Celtic Magic, Ana's next book, is now available.

Want to know how Bree & company got started driving across Death Valley?Join my mailing list at www.linseyhall.com/sub-scribe to get a free copy of *Death Valley Magic*, the story of the Dragon Gods' early adventures. It is available only to newsletter subscribers. Turn the page for an excerpt.

EXCERPT OF DEATH VALLEY MAGIC

Death Valley Junction
   Eight years before the events in Undercover Magic

Getting fired sucked. Especially when it was from a place as crappy as the Death's Door Saloon.

"Don't let the door hit you on the way out," my ex-boss said.

"Screw you, Don." I flipped him the bird and strode out into the sunlight that never gave Death Valley a break.

The door slammed behind me as I shoved on my sunglasses and stomped down the boardwalk with my hands stuffed in my pockets.

What was I going to tell my sisters? We *needed* this job.

There were roughly zero freaking jobs available in this postage stamp town, and I'd just given one up because I wouldn't let the old timers pinch me on the butt when I brought them their beer.

Good going, Ana.

I kicked the dust on the ground and quickened my pace toward home, wondering if Bree and Rowan had heard from Uncle Joe yet. He wasn't blood family—we had none of that left besides each other—but he was the closest thing to it and he'd been missing for three days.

Three days was a lifetime when you were crossing Death Valley. Uncle Joe made the perilous trip about once a month, delivering outlaws to Hider's Haven. It was a dangerous trip on the best of days. But he should have been back by now.

Worry tugged at me as I made the short walk home. Death Valley Junction was a nothing town in the middle of Death Valley, the only all-supernatural city for hundreds of miles. It looked like it was right out of the old west, with low-slung wooden buildings, swinging saloon doors, and boardwalks stretching along the dirt roads.

Our house was at the end of town, a ramshackle thing that had last been repaired in the 1950s. As usual, Bree and Rowan were outside, working on the buggy. The buggy was a monster truck, the type of vehicle used to cross the valley, and it was our pride and joy.

Bree's sturdy boots stuck out from underneath the front of the truck, and Rowan was at the side, painting Ravener poison onto the spikes that protruded from the doors.

"Hey, guys."

Rowan turned. Confusion flashed in her green eyes, and she shoved her black hair back from her cheek. "Oh hell. What happened?"

"Fired." I looked down. "Sorry."

Bree rolled out from under the car. Her dark hair glinted in the sun as she stood, and grease dotted her skin where it was revealed by the strappy brown leather top she wore. We all wore the same style, since it was suited to the climate.

She squinted up at me. "I told you that you should have left that job a long time ago."

"I know. But we needed the money to get the buggy up and running."

She shook her head. "Always the practical one."

"I'll take that as a compliment. Any word from Uncle Joe?"

"Nope." Bree flicked the little crystal she wore around her neck. "He still hasn't activated his panic charm, but he should have been home days ago."

Worry clutched in my stomach. "What if he's wounded and can't activate the charm?"

Months ago, we'd forced him to start wearing the charm. He'd refused initially, saying it didn't matter if we knew he was in trouble. It was too dangerous for us to cross the valley to get him.

But that meant just leaving him. And that was crap, obviously.

We might be young, but we were tough. And we had the buggy. True, we'd never made a trip across, and the truck was only now in working order. But we were gearing up for it. We wanted to join Uncle Joe in the business of transporting outlaws across the valley to Hider's Haven.

He was the only one in the whole town brave enough to make the trip, but he was getting old and we wanted to take over for him. The pay was good. Even better, I wouldn't have to let anyone pinch me on the butt.

There weren't a lot of jobs for girls on the run. We could only be paid under the table, which made it hard.

"Even if he was wounded, Uncle Joe would find a way to activate the charm," Bree said.

As if he'd heard her, the charm around Bree's neck lit up, golden and bright.

She looked down, eyes widening. "Holy fates."

Panic sliced through me. My gaze met hers, then darted to Rowan's. Worry glinted in both their eyes.

"We have to go," Rowan said.

I nodded, my mind racing. This was *real*. We'd only ever

talked about crossing the valley. Planned and planned and planned.

But this was *go time*.

"Is the buggy ready?" I asked.

"As ready as it'll ever be," Rowan said.

My gaze traced over it. The truck was a hulking beast, with huge, sturdy tires and platforms built over the front hood and the back. We'd only ever heard stories of the monsters out in Death Valley, but we needed a place from which to fight them and the platforms should do the job. The huge spikes on the sides would help, but we'd be responsible for fending off most of the monsters.

All of the cars in Death Valley Junction looked like something out of *Mad Max*, but ours was one of the few that had been built to cross the valley.

At least, we hoped it could cross.

We had some magic to help us out, at least. I could create shields, Bree could shoot sonic booms, and Rowan could move things with her mind.

Rowan's gaze drifted to the sun that was high in the sky. "Not the best time to go, but I don't see how we have a choice."

I nodded. No one wanted to cross the valley in the day. According to Uncle Joe, it was the most dangerous of all. But things must be really bad if he'd pressed the button now.

He was probably hoping we were smart enough to wait to cross.

We weren't.

"Let's get dressed and go." I hurried up the creaky front steps and into the ramshackle house.

It didn't take long to dig through my meager possessions and find the leather pants and strappy top that would be my fight wear for out in the valley. It was too hot for anything more, though night would bring the cold.

Daggers were my preferred weapon—mostly since they were cheaper than swords and I had good aim with anything small and pointy. I shoved as many as I could into the little pockets built into the outside of my boots and pants. A small duffel full of daggers completed my arsenal.

I grabbed a leather jacket and the sand goggles that I'd gotten second hand, then ran out of the room. I nearly collided with Bree, whose blue eyes were bright with worry.

"We can do this," I said.

She nodded. "You're right. It's been our plan all along."

I swallowed hard, mind racing with all the things that could go wrong. The valley was full of monsters and dangerous challenges—and according to Uncle Joe, they changed every day. We had no idea what would be coming at us, but we couldn't turn back.

Not with Uncle Joe on the other side.

We swung by the kitchen to grab jugs of water and some food, then hurried out of the house. Rowan was already in the driver's seat, ready to go. Her sand goggles were pushed up on her head, and her leather top looked like armor.

"Get a move on!" she shouted.

I raced to the truck and scrambled up onto the back platform. Though I could open the side door, I was still wary of the Ravener poison Rowan had painted onto the spikes. It would paralyze me for twenty-four hours, and that was the last thing we needed.

Bree scrambled up to join me, and we tossed the supplies onto the floorboard of the back seat, then joined Rowan in the front, sitting on the long bench.

She cranked the engine, which grumbled and roared, then pulled away from the house.

"Holy crap, it's happening." Excitement and fear shivered across my skin.

Worry was a familiar foe. I'd been worried my whole life. Worried about hiding from the unknown people who hunted us. Worried about paying the bills. Worried about my sisters. But it'd never done me any good. So I shoved aside my fear for Uncle Joe and focused on what was ahead.

The wind tore through my hair as Rowan drove away from Death Valley Junction, cutting across the desert floor as the sun blazed down. I shielded my eyes, scouting the mountains ahead. The range rose tall, cast in shadows of gray and beige.

Bree pointed to a path that had been worn through the scrubby ground. "Try here!"

Rowan turned right, and the buggy cut toward the mountains. There was a parallel valley—the *real* Death Valley— that only supernaturals could access. That was what we had to cross.

Rowan drove straight for one of the shallower inclines, slowing the buggy as it climbed up the mountain. The big tires dug into the ground, and I prayed they'd hold up. We'd built most of the buggy from secondhand stuff, and there was no telling what was going to give out first.

The three of us leaned forward as we neared the top, and I swore I could hear our heartbeats pounding in unison. When we crested the ridge and spotted the valley spread out below us, my breath caught.

It was beautiful. And terrifying. The long valley had to be at least a hundred miles long and several miles wide. Different colors swirled across the ground, looking like they simmered with heat.

Danger cloaked the place, dark magic that made my skin crawl.

"Welcome to hell," Bree muttered.

"I kinda like it," I said. "It's terrifying but..."

"Awesome," Rowan said.

"You are both nuts," Bree said. "Now drive us down there. I'm ready to fight some monsters."

Rowan saluted and pulled the buggy over the mountain ridge, then navigated her way down the mountainside.

"I wonder what will hit us first?" My heart raced at the thought.

"Could be anything," Bree said. "Bad Water has monsters, kaleidoscope dunes has all kinds of crazy shit, and the arches could be trouble."

We were at least a hundred miles from Hider's Haven, though Uncle Joe said the distances could change sometimes. Anything could come at us in that amount of time.

Rowan pulled the buggy onto the flat ground.

"I'll take the back." I undid my seatbelt and scrambled up onto the back platform.

Bree climbed onto the front platform, carrying her sword.

"Hang on tight!" Rowan cried.

I gripped the safety railing that we'd installed on the back platform and crouched to keep my balance. She hit the gas, and the buggy jumped forward.

Rowan laughed like a loon and drove us straight into hell.

Up ahead, the ground shimmered in the sun, glowing silver.

"What do you think that is?" Rowan called.

"I don't know," I shouted. "Go around!"

She turned left, trying to cut around the reflective ground, but the silver just extended into our path, growing wider and wider. Death Valley moving to accommodate us.

Moving to trap us.

Then the silver raced toward us, stretching across the ground.

There was no way around.

"You're going to have to drive over it!" I shouted.

She hit the gas harder, and the buggy sped up. The reflective surface glinted in the sun, and as the tires passed over it, water kicked up from the wheels.

"It's the Bad Water!" I cried.

The old salt lake was sometimes dried up, sometimes not. But it wasn't supposed to be deep. Six inches, max. Right?

Please be right, Uncle Joe.

Rowan sped over the water, the buggy's tires sending up silver spray that sparkled in the sunlight. It smelled like rotten eggs, and I gagged, then breathed shallowly through my mouth.

Magic always had a signature—taste, smell, sound. Something that lit up one of the five senses. Maybe more.

And a rotten egg stink was bad news. That meant dark magic.

Tension fizzed across my skin as we drove through the Bad Water. On either side of the car, water sprayed up from the wheels in a dazzling display that belied the danger of the situation. By the time the explosion came, I was strung so tight that I almost leapt off the platform.

The monster was as wide as the buggy, but so long that I couldn't see where it began or ended. It was a massive sea creature with fangs as long as my arm and brilliant blue eyes. Silver scales were the same color as the water, which was still only six inches deep, thank fates.

Magic propelled the monster, who circled our vehicle, his body glinting in the sun. He had to be a hundred feet long, with black wings and claws. He climbed on the ground and leapt into the air, slithering around as he examined us.

"It's the Unhcegila!" Bree cried from the front.

Shit.

Uncle Joe had told us about the Unhcegila—a terrifying water monster from Dakota and Lakota Sioux legends.

Except it was real, as all good legends were. And it occasionally appeared when the Bad Water wasn't dried up. It only needed a few inches to appear.

Looked like it was our lucky day.

My heart thundered as the beast circled, undulating in the air in that signature snakey way. Its eyes pierced me as it waited to strike, and I raised my hands, ready for it.

"Use your shield!" Bree shouted.

"I've got to time it!" I didn't have an endless supply of magic, and wasting it at the beginning of our crossing was a bad idea.

"How do we defeat it?" Rowan cried. "You can't hold it off forever."

My mind raced. Uncle Joe had said something about that. Something...

The creature struck. Light glinted on its fangs, and its breath smelled like week-old garbage as it hurtled toward me.

"Ana!" Rowan cried.

I stifled a gag and called upon my shield magic, envisioning a protective barrier between me and the beast.

It burst from my hands, shining and white. The monster's head slammed into the shield, so hard the collision vibrated up my arms. My magic faltered, weakening.

Damn it.

I wished I had offensive magic—fire, ice, a sonic boom like Bree.

Instead, I was a shield. Destined to react, not act.

The monster reared back and slammed its head against the shield again. It hit with such force that I went to my knees, my arms trembling from the strain of keeping the shield up.

"Drop it so I can hit him!" Bree screamed.

I cut off my magic gratefully, panting. The shield dropped, and Bree's magic swelled on the air, smelling like cedar and sounding like a whistling wind. She hurled her sonic boom, a massive force that smashed into the monster and drove it backward.

The Unhcegila plowed into the water and skidded in the shallows. I scrambled to my feet.

The Unhcegila was fast, rising upward to strike again. My heart thundered as it charged.

Bree threw her sonic boom again. It blasted past me, making my insides vibrate, but the core of it hit the monster, who flew backward again.

It was up a half second later.

"My power isn't working on him!" Bree cried.

No sooner had the words left her mouth than the Unhcegila was up and charging. It moved so fast, plowing toward the front of the buggy where Bree was stationed, I didn't have time to call on my magic.

She struck out with her sword as she dived toward the front seat. The blade sliced the monster's cheek as she flew into the footwell, crashing down next to Rowan. The Unhcegila's head slammed into the bars protecting the front platform, denting them.

The engine roared as Rowan stepped on the gas, and the buggy jumped forward, shaking the Unhcegila off. Stunned, it slipped down into the water.

Bree scrambled up. "I need a freaking shield."

"No kidding," Rowan said. "We'll add it to the list."

I spun to watch the Unhcegila, who was already rising, ready to attack again. I steadied myself on the back platform as we drove away—I was the only thing between it and my sisters.

I'm not going to let it get them.

Its scales glinted in the light, but there was something at its head that shined brighter. A gem—right between its eyes. A tiny red crystal.

A memory flashed in my mind.

"We have to smash the gem!" I cried.

My memory was hazy, but I swore I remembered Uncle Joe telling us the tale of the Unhcegila. Destroying the gem would kill the beast—for now, at least. It would appear again to another traveler, but if we wanted to get it off our butts, we'd have to destroy that gem. And whoever did would get to keep it, and it would bring good luck.

This was going to be up to me. Bree fought with a sword, and Rowan was driving.

I drew a dagger from my boot. The Unhcegila charged, its breath wafting over me, reeking like hot garbage. It opened its mouth wide, fangs glinting.

I hurled my blade, but the monster dodged, then plowed toward me. Before I could build my shield, Bree threw her sonic boom. It blasted past my left shoulder, sending me flying toward the right. I slammed into the safety rails.

The sonic boom nailed the monster right in the face, and the beast tumbled backward.

"Thanks, Bree!" I pushed off the rails and grabbed another dagger.

The monster was rising, but slower this time. Bree's repeated blasts were working. It was weakening.

This was it. My chance.

I used the monster's slowness to my advantage, throwing my dagger right for its eyes. The blade pierced the crystal, and magical energy exploded outward. It blew my hair back from my face and stole the breath from my lungs.

The Unhcegila disappeared in a burst of silver light. A small red crystal flew up into the air, turning end over end and sparkling like a ruby.

"Turn around!" I screamed.

"Why?" Rowan shouted.

"Because!"

"Great reason!" Rowan yanked the wheel to the right, and the buggy made a sharp U-turn. I clung to the railing, keeping my gaze pinned to the crystal. It hurtled back toward the ground, splashing into the water.

The red gem glowed brightly, and I pointed toward it. "Head for the glow!"

Rowan did as I asked, and I climbed over the side of the platform, clinging to the safety railing. "Slow down!"

As we neared the crystal, Rowan slowed the buggy. The gem gleamed brightly, and I hung low, scooping it out of the water. It was warm in my hand, and I squeezed it tight, scrambling back onto the platform.

"Can we keep going now?" Rowan asked.

"Yep!" I looked at the gem briefly. The center was black where my dagger had hit it, but the rest gleamed red and bright. I wasn't sure if it really was lucky, but I could use all the help I could get, so I shoved it into my pocket.

Rowan cut through the rest of the Bad Water without incident, the silver liquid spraying up around the tires and glinting in the sun.

The buggy cut across the desert as the sun beat down upon us. I shielded my eyes, squinting into the distance. Everything was beige, all different shades. And it all shimmered with danger. The air stank with it.

"You smell that?" Rowan asked.

"Yeah, dark magic." It was the thing that made the desert nearly impassable, and the reason that Hider's Haven was so protected. If you wanted to lie low—like, *really* low—that was the place to do it. It was full of criminals, mostly. But also innocent people who were trying to avoid criminals. Get in trouble with the magical mob? Hider's Haven was the supernatural version of witness protection.

Rowan expertly drove the car around scrub brush and boulders. Up ahead, the air shimmered, making it hard to determine what was coming at us. But the air stank with dark magic and prickled, abrading my skin.

Whatever it was, I knew it'd be bad.

~~~

Join my mailing list at www.linseyhall.com/subscribe to continue the adventure and get a free ebook copy of *Death Valley Magic.* No spam and you can leave anytime!

AUTHOR'S NOTE

Thanks for reading *Crime of Magic!* If you've read any of my previous books, you may have noticed that I have a fondness for including historical places and mythological elements. I did the same with *Crime of Magic*, but in this book, I drew primarily from old fairy tales. There are, of course, the mythological elements, like Ana being a Druid and Muffin being the Cat Sìth (a famous fairy creature from Scottish folklore), but most of this book drew from fairy tales.

It was tremendously fun to play with the old fairy tales in this book. If found that once I went back and read the original tales, that they were different than I'd remembered as a child. One of the strangest was the tale of Snow White. There are actually several old versions of this story, but once I read the version in which the Prince requests Snow's dead body and then carries her back to his castle, I knew I had to use it. In that version, she really does fall out of her coffin as they are making their way through the forest. The shock causes her to spit out the apple and she wakes up. Then she immediately marries the Prince. He must have been one charming, good looking dude. I thought that Snow White deserved better than this (and she deserved a date with her future husband), so I switched it around a bit.

As for Hansel and Gretel, I thought it would be just fabulous for Ana and Lachlan to rescue them. Then I went back to revisit the story and realized that they take care of themselves quite handily!

It was the story of Jack and the Beanstalk that made me think twice, however. As I was reading the story, I realized that the giant really didn't do anything wrong other than stomping around and yelling at Jack, who was stealing from him. Maybe he would have lived up to his promise and eaten Jack, but maybe not. Either way, Jack seemed like a guy who kept robbing the giant and then orchestrating (successfully) his death. He seemed like a bit of a jerk, really. As I read more about the evolution of Jack's tale throughout time (as it was passed down through generations) I realized that other people had issue with this as well. Most often, they retold the story with a slightly different angle. In their modified versions, they made it clear that the giant was a bad guy. One version made the addition of the giant killing Jack's father when he was young. I decided to take another angle on this all together and make Jack the bad guy.

And last—the Big Bad Wolf and the White Rabbit. Both of those were fun modifications that I invented.

I think that's it for the history and mythology in *Crime of Magic*—at least the big things. I hope you enjoyed the book and will come back for more of Ana, Lachlan, Rowan, and Bree!

ACKNOWLEDGMENTS

Thank you, Ben, for everything. There would be no books without you.

Thank you to Orina Kafe for the beautiful cover art. Thank you to Richard for your keen eye on spotting errors, and thank you to Emma for your champagne facts. Thank you to Collette Markwardt for allowing me to borrow the Pugs of Destruction, who are real dogs named Chaos, Havoc, and Ruckus. They were all adopted from rescue agencies.

GLOSSARY

Alpha Council - There are two governments that enforce law for supernaturals—the Alpha Council and the Order of the Magica. The Alpha Council governs all shifters. They work cooperatively with the Alpha Council when necessary—for example, when capturing FireSouls.

Blood Sorcerer - A type of Magica who can create magic using blood.

Dark Magic - The kind that is meant to harm. It's not necessarily bad, but it often is.

Demons - Often employed to do evil. They live in various hells but can be released upon the earth if you know how to get to them and then get them out. If they are killed on Earth, they are sent back to their hell.

Dragon Sense - A FireSoul's ability to find treasure. It is an internal sense that pulls them toward what they seek. It is easiest to find gold, but they can find anything or anyone that is valued by someone.

Djinn - Possesses invisibility and the ability to possess others for brief periods of time.

Earthwalking Gods - Reincarnates of the ancient gods who

can walk upon the earth. They are mortal but with all the power of that god.

Enchanted Artifacts – Artifacts can be imbued with magic that lasts after the death of the person who put the magic into the artifact (unlike a spell that has not been put into an artifact—these spells disappear after the Magica's death). But magic is not stable. After a period of time—hundreds or thousands of years depending on the circumstance—the magic will degrade. Eventually, it can go bad and cause many problems.

Fire Mage – A mage who can control fire.

FireSoul - A very rare type of Magica who shares a piece of the dragon's soul. They can locate treasure and steal the gifts (powers) of other supernaturals. With practice, they can manipulate the gifts they steal, becoming the strongest of that gift. They are despised and feared. If they are caught, they are thrown in the Prison of Magical Deviants.

The Great Peace - The most powerful piece of magic ever created. It hides magic from the eyes of humans.

Magica - Any supernatural who has the power to create magic—witches, sorcerers, mages. All are governed by the Order of the Magica.

Order of the Magica - There are two governments that enforce law for supernaturals—the Alpha Council and the Order of the Magica. The Order of the Magica govern all Magica. They work cooperatively with the Alpha Council when necessary—for example, when capturing FireSouls.

Seeker - A type of supernatural who can find things. FireSouls often pass off their dragon sense as Seeker power.

Shifter - A supernatural who can turn into an animal. All are governed by the Alpha Council.

Transporter - A type of supernatural who can travel anywhere. Their power is limited and must regenerate after each use.

Undercover Protectorate - A secret organization dedicated to protecting supernaturals and solving the crimes that no one else will.

Vampire - Blood drinking supernaturals with great strength and speed who live in a separate realm.

ABOUT LINSEY

Before becoming a writer, Linsey Hall was a nautical archaeologist who studied shipwrecks from Hawaii and the Yukon to the UK and the Mediterranean. She credits fantasy and historical romances with her love of history and her career as an archaeologist. After a decade of tromping around the globe in search of old bits of stuff that people left lying about, she settled down and started penning her own romance novels. Her Dragon's Gift series draws upon her love of history and the paranormal elements that she can't help but include.

COPYRIGHT